Attain Walsh knew something was odd at Nicholas Lindson's ranch. Ever since his best friend married Sandra, things have turned . . . strange. Wanting to get to the bottom of things, Attain begins to show up unexpectedly. He's shocked to stumble across Nicholas making out with someone other than his wife. The idea that his buddy was a cheat had never crossed his mind. Unable to help himself, Attain confronts Nicholas . . . and learns that the marriage is a sham. Both Nicholas and Sandra have separate partners. Not only that, but his friend's partner—Bodb—isn't human. He's a gargoyle. When Attain meets more of them, he's shocked to find himself attracted to one of the huge beasts—a dark-blue gargoyle named Ssimeas. Then he learns about mates—someone the gargoyle considers the other half of their soul—and Ssimeas claims that Attain is his. But Attain is a confirmed bachelor. He has no desire to be anyone's soul mate. Can Attain convince the gargoyle to leave him alone? Or will the male's flattering pursuit sway him into turning his life upside down?

This book is a work of fiction. Names, characters, places, and incidents either are products of the author's imagination or are used fictitiously. Any resemblance to actual events or locales or persons, living or dead, is entirely coincidental.

The Bachelor Thief
Copyright © 2019 Charlie Richards
ISBN: 978-1-4874-2742-9
Cover art by Angela Waters

Published by eXtasy Books Inc or
Devine Destinies, an imprint of eXtasy Books Inc

Look for us online at:
www.eXtasybooks.com or www.devinedestinies.com

THE BACHELOR THIEF
A PARANORMAL'S LOVE : BOOK TWENTY-EIGHT

BY

CHARLIE RICHARDS

Dedication

To those readers who were curious how gargoyles handle birth control when cinnamon isn't an option. This one's for you all.

You stole my heart, but I'll let you keep it.
~Unknown

CHAPTER ONE

Something fishy was going on at Nicholas Lindson's ranch. Attain Walsh felt certain of it. Ever since his best friend had married Sandra and moved full time to his ranch, things had . . . changed.

Attain could have chalked it up to Nicholas and Sandra building a life together. Except, whenever he dropped by the ranch, he never saw Sandra. When Attain asked after her, Nicholas would smile, laugh, and offer some excuse as to her absence.

On top of that, Attain had spotted a lot of new ranch hands. He had also been introduced to an older man named Bodb — no last name offered. Nicholas had claimed he was a cattle rancher from Montana who was studying the differences between their state's practices.

Never heard a bigger fish story in my life.

Lifting the TV remote, Attain clicked the button. He wasn't watching it anyway. After setting the remote aside, he rose to his feet and stretched his arms overhead. Attain twisted this way and that until he felt a satisfying pop in his lower back.

"Gotcha," Attain muttered.

Attain had been spending way too many hours in a chair behind his desk. As an attorney, long hours were expected, but recently, his father had been piling on the work. He was barely keeping up even when pulling twelve-hour shifts.

Lowering his arms, Attain grabbed his beer bottle. He swigged back the last of it, trying to dispel the memory of his meeting with his father that evening. It didn't work.

As Attain had been headed out of the office, George Walsh had called, "Attain, come into my office before you leave."

Knowing an order when he heard one, Attain had changed directions and obeyed. He hadn't immediately sat, hoping whatever it was his father needed would be brief.

George had leaned back in his desk chair, steepled his fingers, and eyed him for a few seconds. "Now that Nicholas has settled down, have you thought about following suit?" He lifted one dark-brown eyebrow imperiously, as if daring Attain to give him the wrong answer.

Good grief. Not this again.

Attain mentally groaned, but he kept his annoyance off his face. What was it with parents meddling in their kids' personal lives? Instead, Attain grinned broadly and waggled his eyebrows, hoping to instill levity in what he knew George expected to be a serious conversation.

"Afraid not, Father." Attain shoved his hands into his suit pants pockets and forced a soft chuckle. "I'm like you when you were my age." Twisting his grin into a roguish smile, he winked. "A confirmed bachelor. Too much work and too many gorgeous ladies to enjoy the company of."

George's eyes narrowed, and the lines around his lips tightened. "And I also told you that when I did marry your mother, it was the best decision I ever made."

Attain smiled, thinking of his deceased mother. "Yeah. Mom was special." Even as she excelled at being the perfect social wife, she'd still managed to be a warm and caring mother. "One of a kind." Attain sighed, dipping his chin as he met his father's brown eyes, so different from his own, since he'd inherited his mother's clear baby blues. "I'm waiting until I find that special lady like you did."

Hearing his father's soft harrumph, Attain hoped the conversation was over.

He wasn't so lucky.

George rested his hands on the arms of his large chair and asked, "What about that Chrissy Alderman? She's a lovely lady and seemed quite keen on you at Nicholas's wedding. Have you taken the time to get to know her better?"

Attain racked his brain for a suitable response that wouldn't cause his father to chastise him for besmirching a young lady's honor. "Uh—" *Real eloquent, Attain. Get your head in it.* After clearing his throat, Attain hurriedly commented, "No, Father. You know how busy we are right now."

He realized work probably wasn't the greatest excuse, but it was the best he'd been able to come up with when put on the spot by his father.

"I thought as much," George commented, nodding. "I'll give this new case to Edward, so when you finish the Buckwater and Stewardship cases this week and next, you'll have some time freed up." Then he gave Attain a wide smile that sent Attain's internal alarm pinging. "In fact, come over Saturday evening for dinner." George rose from his chair and picked up his suit jacket, pulling it on as he continued speaking. "Drinks at six-thirty."

As if Attain didn't already know that.

Attain just knew his father was up to something, but he couldn't refuse. "I'll be there," he promised, even though it was the last thing he wanted to do. "What will Candice be serving?" Attain asked, referring to George's cook.

Turning, Attain headed toward the door when he saw him pick up his briefcase. As he walked with George out of their offices, locking up behind them, they chatted about Candice's planned dinner. His mouth watered at the prospect of enjoying her pot roast and apple turnovers for dessert.

Sighing deeply, Attain finally managed to pull himself into the here and now. He decided if he was going to spend Saturday evening with his father, talking about work, he was going to have a little fun earlier that day. Attain smiled evilly as he grabbed another beer.

"Plus, me showing up at the ranch unannounced on a Saturday morning is the last thing Nicholas will expect."

With that thought floating through his mind, Attain headed to his home office to finish some reading he'd been putting off.

Attain drove his *Chevy Avalanche* down Nicholas's ranch's driveway. Glancing left and right, he took a moment to admire his buddy's ranch. Normally, he had to focus on the gravel road, since he usually drove his *Ducati* when visiting the man.

The change in engine noise was another part of his plan.

I really want to know what the hell is going on out here.

If Attain wasn't so worried about what was going on with his best friend, he would feel guilty about popping in this way. On more than one occasion, Nicholas had teased, "I always know it's you because I can hear you come roaring down my driveway from a mile away."

Using his *Avalanche* meant Nicholas wouldn't know it was him. Instead, he could be any one of a dozen ranch hands returning from a fun Friday night.

Attain parked in front of the main house and took a long look around. Leaning forward, he spotted movement in the shadows of the second-floor hayloft. While the door was open, he couldn't make out anything but the fact that whoever was up there was big and broad.

Huh.

Not wanting his cover blown, Attain quickly exited his vehicle. He strode up the four porch steps and crossed the front porch. Reaching the door, he only hesitated a moment to grab the handle and open the door.

Even as Attain slipped inside, he dismissed the butterflies in his gut. He heard the rumble of voices and followed the sound. Pausing in the doorway of the expansive dining room, he expected to see the group finishing up breakfast.

It seemed he had just missed it.

In fact, upon seeing the scene unfolding before him, shock rocked Attain's body. His jaw sagged open, and his eyes widened. He blinked once, twice, just to make certain the scene wouldn't change.

It didn't.

Attain saw Albert Lindson—Nicholas's uncle, who had been estranged for a few years and had recently returned to the ranch—grab the hand of a slender, auburn-haired, and much younger-looking man. Albert smirked and shook his head as he glanced to his left before leading the stranger out of the room.

The low rumble of masculine groans returned Attain's focus to what Albert had walked away from—with amusement.

Nicholas was pinned against the wall by Bodb . . . and they were making out. With his arms around the larger, older man's shoulders, his buddy obviously welcomed the attention. Bodb's hand threading through Nicholas's hair appeared to be encouraging him to tip his head just right, while he began shoving his left hand under his friend's shirt.

What the fucking hell?

His buddy had gotten married less than two months before. Where was Sandra? Did she know about Nicholas's . . . friend? Nicholas and Sandra had been together for years.

Why would he do this to her?

Attain had never considered the idea that Nicholas could be a cheater, but the proof was right before his eyes.

For an instant, Attain thought about backing away. He could go to the front door and knock. He could pretend he didn't know.

Except, I can't. I came to get answers, and I want them, dammit.

After managing to shut his trap, Attain cleared his throat. To his surprise, it took him doing that two more times before

Bodb pulled away from Nicholas. The gray-haired man turned his head, and one brow lifted.

Attain noticed there wasn't a hint of remorse in his expression.

Nicholas, on the other hand, his features flushed pink when he met Attain's gaze.

"You know," Attain murmured, finding his voice. "I'd thought something weird was going on with you for a while." Rubbing the back of his neck with one hand, he waved his other at the pair who still stood in each other's arms. "But I sure never woulda thought it was this." He shook his head as he muttered, "I didn't even realize you were into guys."

Bodb turned and gazed down at Nicholas, a smile toying at the edges of his kiss-swollen lips. "You did tell me you thought we should share the truth with Attain."

Nicholas nodded. "I did." Then he chuckled as he eased from Bodb's arms. "Not the way I thought it would happen, but—" He shrugged, the color easing from his cheeks as he waved toward the table. "Bodb will get us all coffee. Have a seat."

To Attain's continuing surprise, Nicholas tipped his face up, and Bodb pressed a quick peck to his lips before heading through the swinging door that led to the kitchen.

"Shit, man," Attain hissed, grabbing the back of a chair and yanking it out. Discomfort flooded him as he plopped onto it. "What the fuck?"

Nicholas settled at the table across from him. Resting his hands on the table, he rubbed over the dark wood. "Does me kissing a man disgust you that much?"

So not the question I thought he'd ask.

"No," Attain burst out, scowling at his friend. "I couldn't give a shit that Bodb is a guy." Rolling his eyes, he snapped, "It's the fact that you're cheating on Sandra . . . and you've been married less than two months." Attain scoffed as he scowled at Nicholas. "What happened, man? You know I never settled down to date anyone because I have an issue with that. Not after — "

Snapping his mouth shut, Attain shook his head. He was not going to think about her. Attain continued to glare at Nicholas, uncertain what else to say without sounding like an asshole.

"Ah."

How Nicholas made that one word sound so damn understanding, Attain had no idea. When Nicholas reached across the table and rested his fingertips on Attain's clenched hand, Attain jolted in his seat.

"I'm sorry, Attain," Nicholas murmured. "I should have remembered how sensitive you are to cheating." After tapping the back of his clenched fist, he added, "That's not what's happening here. I assure you."

After sucking in a deep breath, Attain let it out slowly. At the same time, he eased his hand away and placed his palms flat on the table. "Okay." Attain held Nicholas's gaze, seeing the concern in his dark-brown eyes. "So what's going on here?"

"Okay, well . . ." Nicholas straightened in his seat as Bodb entered carrying three mugs. The two in his right hand he placed on his and Nicholas's side of the table. Bodb reached over and put the third mug before Attain. "Thanks, Bodb," Nicholas stated, grabbing a cup and cradling it between his palms.

Bodb nodded, then settled beside Nicholas.

Nicholas cleared his throat, then asked, "At the wedding, did you notice how bigoted Sandra's father was toward Mitch and his partner?"

While Attain didn't know what it had to do with anything, he nodded. "Kinda hard not to."

The man had never met a cliché he hadn't embraced.

"Well, Sandra is a lesbian. She's been in a relationship with a woman named Maggie for several years." Nicholas threaded his fingers through Bodb's, a wry smile curving his lips. "I agreed to be her beard, and she didn't care who I fucked as long as I was discreet." Then Nicholas gazed at Bodb. "Then on the trip with Baltus to track down Mitch, I met Bodb, and—" His smile turned sappy-looking as he held the older man's gaze. "Well, Bodb understood my situation, and he's been patient about it while we wait for Sandra to decide it's time to come out." Nicholas returned his focus to Attain, a happy light gleaming in his eyes. "His patience has paid off because that time was just last week. Sandra and I are getting an annulment, but we didn't want to tell anyone until it went through."

Gaping, Attain stared at Nicholas for a long minute, waiting for more. There had to be more, right? However, Nicholas just smiled at him and sipped his coffee.

Attain lifted his mug to his lips and drank deeply of the dark, bitter brew. Grimacing, he set it down and reached for the glass sugar decanter in the middle of the table. During those few precious seconds it took to doctor his coffee, Attain swiftly processed everything his best friend had said.

There's still more. There has to be.

Nicholas and Sandra having separate relationships didn't explain the extra wranglers—big men who looked a whole lot like security or guards.

Focusing on Bodb, Attain narrowed his eyes. "You're still hiding something," he declared, deciding to be blunt. "What's with the bodyguards in disguise? Are they your men?"

Bodb nodded as he smirked. "They *are* my men."

"Told you Attain was observant," Nicholas stated around a snicker.

"Indeed you did." Bodb gripped his coffee mug in his left hand while slinging his right arm around Nicholas's shoulders. He threaded his fingers through Nicholas's hair, petting him. "Do you think it's safe to share everything with him?"

Nicholas nodded once. "I told you we would have to eventually," he reminded.

Bodb sighed deeply. "I know. I had just hoped to be able to put it off as long as possible." His thick lips twisted into a grimace. "Telling outsiders is dangerous."

"Attain isn't, though," Nicholas insisted, reaching over and squeezing Bodb's thigh. "I'm sure."

Scowling, confusion and concern flooding him, Attain leaned forward and tapped the table with his forefingers. "Hello. Sitting right here." His belligerent comment drew both men's attention. Attain focused a hard look at Bodb. "Did you drag Nicholas into something illegal? Something dangerous? Because if you did, I'll—"

"Just stop, Attain," Nicholas countered, lifting his hand palm out. "It's not like that."

"Then what's it like?" Attain glanced between them, trying to read Nicholas's expression, but all he saw was amusement. "What's so funny?"

Grinning broadly, Nicholas waggled his brows as he leaned forward, resting his forearms on the table. "You know how whenever someone tries to explain something unbelievable, they always start with . . . now I know how crazy this sounds, but I swear it's true?"

"Yeah?" Attain murmured, cocking his head. Just what was his buddy going to tell him?

"Well." Nicholas rubbed the back of his neck as he cleared his throat. He turned his attention to Bodb. "Now, I realize how hard this was for Mitch to explain to me."

Bodb chuckled as he grinned. "I could do a little show and tell first."

Nicholas rolled his eyes. "That would just freak him out."

Attain huffed a sigh. "What the hell, man?" He waved his hand in a *go ahead* motion. "Just blurt it out already."

"Okay." Nicholas tipped his chin in a quick nod. "Paranormals are real." He jutted his thumb toward Bodb. "This is Elder Bodb, a leader of the gargoyle race, and I'm his mate." Pointing toward the back door, Nicholas added, "Those big men you see wandering around. Those are his security, gargoyle enforcers."

Glancing between the pair, Attain waited for the punch line. Then the reason Nicholas prefaced his explanation with — *I know how crazy this sounds* — hit him. His buddy actually believed what he said.

Nicholas patted Bodb's thigh. "Okay. Now time for the show and tell part."

Bodb nodded and rose to his feet.

Attain watched as Bodb stripped off his shirt and kicked off his boots. He glanced at Nicholas, who held up his index finger in a *wait a sec* gesture. Gritting his teeth, Attain returned his focus to Bodb . . . just in time to see . . . something . . .

Bodb's skin had changed, darkened, and taken on a distinctively purple hue. He grew taller, larger, broader . . . his jaw squarer, and —

"What. The. Fuck?" Attain roared the words as he leaped to his feet.

CHAPTER TWO

Ssimeas came out of roost swiftly, as he always did. He started to rise from the crouch he traditionally rested in. Sighing, he flopped onto his butt and looked around the space.

Life sure has changed in the last several months.

Rubbing his dark-blue hand over his bald pate, Ssimeas smiled. He chuckled as he peered around the clean, well-ordered loft of the barn. The place where he and a couple of other gargoyles roosted — slept as a stone statue during daylight hours, or for the mated ones, when they needed to enjoy their weekly recharge — was tucked behind a high wall of hay bales. It was secluded and dark, with several comfortable pallets laid out.

That had been Nicholas's idea.

Ssimeas chuckled upon thinking of Elder Bodb's mate's thoughtfulness. At a look from his elder, Ssimeas had bit back his comment of, "Why? We're stone while roosting and can't exactly feel comfort."

That thought returned Ssimeas to how life had changed.

At almost a millennium, he'd spent the last three hundred plus years working as an enforcer for the Circle of Elders — the dozen oldest and wisest of their kind. Only five of the twelve elders had been mated until Bodb had met Nicholas. Due to the human's responsibilities to his family and friends, Bodb hadn't been able to whisk him away immediately.

Instead, the elder was living as a human businessman with his partner on a cattle ranch. That meant he needed security.

Ssimeas, having noticed over the centuries that where Fate provided one mate, more often followed, had asked to be assigned to him.

His wish had been granted.

And that's why I roost in a barn's hayloft every day.

Ssimeas laughed softly as he rose to his feet and stretched his arms over his head. Threading his fingers, he twisted and arched. Grunting softly, he spread his black wings, the tips brushing the sloped ceiling.

His stomach rumbled. Lowering his hands, he rubbed at his abdominals, wondering what Pauline was whipping up for himself and Biscane. Pauline was a fox shifter and mated to another gargoyle, Lebone. When she'd arrived, she'd taken over the kitchen duties. Prior to that, it had been handled by the housekeeper—Shandell.

Soon after, Shandell had retired to live with her daughter in Florida. She'd explained that she'd only stayed on because she'd been worried about how Nicholas would care for himself if she wasn't there. Of course, then she'd patted Nicholas on the cheek and told him, "But now you have your wife, Sandra, her friend, Maggie, and a cook, and all these other people to help around here."

Nicholas hadn't corrected her.

When Ssimeas's stomach growled again, he bent his knees, flapped his wings, and lunged toward the top of the six-high stack of hay bales. He easily landed on top of them in a crouch. Crawling across the top of the stack, he turned his thoughts to Biscane.

His fellow unmated gargoyle should have woken from roost with him.

So where the fuck is he?

He and Biscane were unmated guards, taking the night shift, watching over Elder Bodb, Nicholas, and the ranch most of the evening. Lebone and Sindrid—another mated gargoyle—could change to human form, so they handled the day shift. Last Ssimeas had heard, Bodb's brothers—Gladstone and Lludd—one mated and one not, respectively—would soon be joining them to round out the half dozen guards.

Ssimeas looked forward to the break.

"Speaking of breaks," Ssimeas muttered as he reached the edge of the haystack and dropped onto the loft floor. "Seems Biscane finally convinced Redfeather to enjoy a romp with him."

There were a few of Nicholas's most trusted hands that knew the truth of who Elder Bodb was as well as how Sandra's significant other, Maggie, was actually a witch. Not to mention how there were several vampires on the property. Stanley Redfeather, the ranch foreman, was one of those people. The handsome Native American had been turning down Biscane for months.

So what changed his mind?

Ssimeas could only guess. Reaching the open loft doors, he spotted Biscane's big form exiting the bunkhouse.

Huh. Guess he didn't snag Redfeather's attention after all.

Ssimeas wondered which of the wranglers Biscane had bedded. There were three of the six that knew of paranormals. When they'd arrived, they'd been surprised to discover that one of the wranglers was actually a cougar shifter—Virgil McBride.

Virgil had been instrumental in letting them know which of the wranglers could handle the truth of paranormals and who had to be left in the dark.

Shaking his head, Ssimeas swept his gaze over the rest of the yard. He took in the shadows created by the buildings and saw the animals dozing in pens and paddocks. Listening, he heard the noises from the barn beneath his feet—the nicker of horses, the thud of their hooves, and the crunch of them eating their hay.

Everything seemed peaceful.

Ssimeas's rumbling stomach pulled his focus to the main

ranch house. Stepping out of the loft door, he used his wings to control his descent to the ground. Once he'd landed, he wrapped his large black appendages around his shoulders.

Sticking to the shadows, Ssimeas took his time rounding the buildings. Unlike some other gargoyles, who could use hats and fake beards to disguise their features in the dark, he didn't have that luxury. His large black horns would give him away every time ... so he remained vigilant to avoid strangers.

Reaching the front of the main house — it was easier to go in the front door, since it was shielded from most prying eyes — Ssimeas paused and cocked his head. He took in the dark vehicle parked to the left of the front door. Not recognizing the *Avalanche*, he headed toward it.

Ssimeas rounded the vehicle, searching for clues as to the owner. The front, driver's side window was open, and he dipped his head inside it. As he swept his gaze over the impressively clean interior, Ssimeas inhaled deeply.

An earthy masculine aroma teased his senses, causing his gut to clench and his blood to heat. Gasping in surprise, he filled his lungs with another breath of the delicious aroma. His cock plumped inside his loincloth.

Jerking back in surprise, Ssimeas caught his horn on the edge of the window. "Shit," he muttered as discomfort shot down his neck. Rolling his eyes, Ssimeas corrected his angle and pulled his head out of the SUV. "Such a hatchling move."

"What are you grumbling about, Ssimeas?" Biscane's deep voice held a note of teasing. "You upset because you didn't get any like I did last night?"

As Ssimeas watched, Biscane reached down and cupped the crotch of his loincloth.

Shaking his head, Ssimeas sniffed none-too-discreetly. "You know LeeAnn is looking for a relationship, right?" He'd scented the arousal of the skilled female wrangler when she'd seen Biscane a time or two while making his rounds in passing. "She has a crush on you. Be careful."

Biscane's jaw sagged open, and his black eyebrow ridges shot up. "B-But she's not m-my mate." He shook his head as he rubbed the back of his neck, betraying his discomfort with his actions along with his scent. "We were just having fun."

Ssimeas grunted, his focus straying back to the *Avalanche*. "Better make sure she knows that, or you could have a problem on your hands." Without waiting for his fellow gargoyle's response, he pointed at the SUV and asked, "Do you know whose this is?"

Nodding, Biscane held up his cell phone. "Attain is here."

"Attain?" Ssimeas felt his gut clench upon hearing the name. "I thought he rode a *Ducati*."

"Yeah. Got a text from Sindrid that Attain is here. Guess he uses this around town," Biscane told him as he headed toward the porch. "Ready for breakfast?"

Nodding absently, Ssimeas followed, trying to work out what his responses were telling him in conjunction with what he knew about Attain. It sort of made sense. Any time he'd heard the distinctive roar of the *Ducati*'s engine, Ssimeas had stayed away from the house.

My mate has been under my nose for months, and I didn't realize it.

"Sindrid said we could enter even though he's here?" Last Ssimeas had heard, they hadn't told Attain about paranormals, yet. A heartbeat later, he murmured absently, "Of course, if he's my mate, that'll have to change."

"Yeah. Nicholas and Bodb told Attain this morning. He's been here all day." Biscane pulled open the front door, lowering his voice as he added, "Guess he's struggling with it a little. Hey, did you just say he's your mate?"

Lifting his clawed hands, Ssimeas hissed, "Keep it down." Another thought occurred to him. "Maybe it was someone who rode in his *Avalanche* recently."

Biscane nodded, lowering his voice as he held the door open for Ssimeas. "I hope that's the case for you, Ssim." His black features twisted into a grimace. "Because I haven't heard anything from anyone that indicates Attain is interested in settling down . . . or that he's gay or bisexual."

Unfortunately, Ssimeas had heard those things, too.

Even as Ssimeas nodded, he dipped his head so his horns would clear the doorway as he entered. Then he inhaled deeply, parsing out the different scents. Elder Bodb's, Nicholas's, Sandra's, and Maggie's all hung heavy in the air, as did Lebone's and Pauline's. Even Vernon—Nicholas's half-brother's—lingered lightly in the air, telling Ssimeas that he'd passed through the house not too long ago. While Vernon had been staying at the ranch for the last week and a half, they had so far managed to keep the existence of paranormals from the man. The final scent that permeated the rooms was the same as the one in the *Avalanche*.

Attain Walsh is my mate.

Ssimeas paused to inhale deeply, a shiver working up his spine. His gut clenched, and he swallowed hard. He paused before the turn needed to head into the dining room, clenching and unclenching his fists.

Gods, I'm about to meet my destiny, and I'm standing here like a wuss.

To Ssimeas's surprise, Biscane stopped next to him. "Elder Bodb," Biscane called respectfully as he knocked on the doorframe. "Is it safe to enter?"

"It is," Lebone answered. "They have Attain getting drunk in the family room." As both Biscane and Ssimeas started moving again, rounding the corner to enter the dining room, Lebone added, "Come get dinner before starting your shift."

"Attain is my mate."

If Ssimeas could have blushed, he would have. Still, upon seeing Lebone's jaw sag open, he felt his cheeks heat a little.

"Really?" Lebone cocked his head. "Damn. Okay."

"You're sure, then, huh?" Biscane rested his fists on his hips as he met his gaze. When Ssimeas nodded, he grinned widely, showing off his sharp teeth. "Well, congrats, man." Biscane shoved him on his shoulder. "I've seen Attain from afar. He's a good lookin' man."

"Attain *is* good looking," Pauline commented, rolling a three-tiered cart through the swinging door that led to the ranch house's expansive kitchen. She and Lebone lived in a large suite that was attached to the kitchen's other side. "And a little frazzled right now." As Pauline glanced around the room, she smiled at them all. "Why are we talking about the poor dear?"

Poor dear? If Pauline is referring to Attain like that then — "He's not taking learning of paranormals well, is he?"

"Afraid not," Lebone confirmed. Wrapping his arm around Pauline's waist, he told her, "Ssimeas believes Attain is his mate."

"Oh!" Pauline beamed at him. "Then that should help, right?"

"Only if he accepts him." Biscane began removing the food from the tray and spreading it on the table.

Lebone smacked the black gargoyle upside the head. "Tact, man," he grumbled when Biscane shot a surprised look the human-looking gargoyle's way. Shaking his head, Lebone turned his attention on Ssimeas. "You want to eat first? Or meet him?"

Ssimeas's stomach rumbled. "You mind if I take a few of those sausage, egg, and cheese sandwiches into the family room?" Even as he asked, he grabbed a paper plate and began loading several on it. "I need to at least see him."

"You know they're pretty zen about people eating in the family room." Lebone chuckled as he crossed to the coffee service resting on the sideboard. "Otherwise, how could Sandra and Maggie eat all that popcorn and sugary snacks while watching their chick flicks?"

"Hey, I resemble that remark," a feminine voice stated, announcing Sandra and Maggie's arrival into the dining room. She flicked her long blonde ponytail over her shoulder as she arched her perfectly manicured left eyebrow. "We all know how you love to join us, and you eat your fair share of popcorn and gumdrops."

Lebone laughed as he rubbed his belly. "Love those damn things." Then he sobered as he poured hot water into a mug. After adding a tea bag of Earl Grey, Lebone crossed to Ssimeas and held it out to him. After Ssimeas took it, he said, "Well, let's go introduce you to Attain, then. We need to tell Elder Bodb of this development anyway."

"Why are you—" Sandra began, then paused and glanced blatantly at Ssimeas's groin—and obviously spotted the bulge there. She reached out and threaded her fingers with Maggie's. "Mates?" When Ssimeas nodded, she used her free hand to squeeze his forearm. "Go slow. Attain won't appreciate being steamrolled."

Ssimeas nodded. "Thank you."

Seeing as Sandra had known the man for years, Ssimeas intended to take that advice to heart. He followed Lebone to the closed French doors and waited while his fellow enforcer knocked. Tension thrummed through him, mixing with anticipation, causing his gut to churn.

Ssimeas wasn't certain he would be able to eat, after all.

Don't want to pass out, though.

"Something I can help you with, Lebone?" Elder Bodb asked quietly from where he'd eased one of the sliding doors open a couple of inches. The elder's gaze drifted to Ssimeas. "Is there an issue?"

With his mouth dry, Ssimeas couldn't manage to answer.

Fortunately, Lebone did it for him. "Yes, Elder," he murmured, tipping his chin in Ssimeas's direction. "It seems this is the first Ssimeas has caught Attain's scent." When Elder

Bodb just lifted one brow in silent question, Lebone added, "He's certain Attain is his mate."

Elder Bodb's dark-gray eyebrows shot up, and he pinned Ssimeas with a pointed stare. "Really?"

Ssimeas nodded. "He'd always come here on his *Ducati*, and I knew to stay away, so I never scented him before." He swallowed hard as he glanced beyond the elder, eager to see his mate up close. "He's mine."

"Congratulations, old friend," Elder Bodb murmured, giving him a warm smile. "This wooing might take some time," he warned. "But Fate is never wrong." After that cryptic comment, Elder Bodb took a step backward and opened the door wider. "Come in."

"Thank you."

Ssimeas did as he'd been instructed and strode slowly into the room. As he peered around the large space, he heard the door slide closed behind him. His gaze landed on the light-brown-haired man he'd never officially met—Attain Walsh.

Taking in the handsome, masculine beauty that was his mate, Ssimeas admired his strong lines. He had a fairly lean build with muscular limbs, showcased by his short-sleeved polo shirt and his form-fitting jeans. His wide lips were parted in obvious surprise as he gazed back at Ssimeas, and he noticed the slight sheen filling his pale blue eyes that could probably be from shock or the alcohol he was drinking.

Ssimeas had to fight back the urge to go over there, sit down next to the man on the sofa, take him in his arms, and delve his tongue between those parted lips.

"Uh, Bodb. I thought we weren't doing any more show and tell today."

Nicholas's comment yanked Ssimeas out of his lustful musings, and he focused on the elder's human.

"Something has come up, handsome," Elder Bodb stated as he settled on the love seat next to Nicholas and wrapped his arm around his shoulders. "Do you remember how we stopped shy of explaining mates to Attain?" After Nicholas had nodded, Bodb waved his hand toward Ssimeas as he stated, "This is the first time Ssimeas has scented Attain, and now we have to change that."

Nicholas's eyes widened as he glanced between them. "Oh."

"Well, congrats, Ssimeas." That was from the vampire Spieron. He was part of the other couple in the room, sitting with his beloved, Albert. The vampire grinned widely at him, his fangs on clear display.

Evidently, the group had explained more than just gargoyles to Attain.

No wonder he's overwhelmed.

"What the fuck is going on?"

The melodious tenor of his mate's voice caused a wash of heat to flood Ssimeas's veins. Once again, he fought the desire to rush to the man and take him in his arms.

Gods, going slow is going to be damn tough.

Pulling on every bit of his nearly a millennia of hard-won self-control, Ssimeas moved slowly as he headed to the big sofa Attain sat on. He settled on the opposite corner before placing his food and drink on the coffee table before him. Finally, Ssimeas turned and held out his clawed hand to Attain.

"Hello, Attain. I'm Ssimeas, one of the elder's enforcers."

Then, with bated breath, Ssimeas waited to see if he would be granted his mate's first touch.

CHAPTER THREE

Attain didn't understand the sudden desire to touch the massive creature—gargoyle—who'd sat on the sofa beside him. In fact, it scared him. He certainly hadn't reacted that way when Bodb, Lebone, and Sindrid had revealed their true forms to him.

Not completely beside me, but definitely near enough to touch. And he's holding out his hand. Shit!

When the moment dragged, and Attain didn't take Ssimeas's hand, the gargoyle's brow ridges furrowed. That was what Bodb had called them. Seeing the concern fill his deep gray eyes and how his shoulders drooped just a little as he began to lower his hand spurred Attain into action.

Attain reached out and gripped Ssimeas's much-larger hand. Feeling the slightly swarthy skin against his palm, he felt his heart race in his chest. Tingles erupted on his forearm, causing his hairs to stand on end.

What the hell?

"I'm very pleased to meet you, Attain," Ssimeas stated softly, squeezing Attain's hand lightly as he rubbed his thumb over the back of it. Before Attain could question him or protest, Ssimeas released him. "I just woke from roost, so I hope you don't mind if I eat while we chat."

"Uhhh . . ."

Attain snapped his mouth shut while glancing at the food and drink Ssimeas had placed on the coffee table. He recalled Bodb telling him that roost was the gargoyles' version of REM sleep. In fact, until a gargoyle bonded, they were forced to roost as a stone statue during daylight hours.

Right. That means he's hungry.

Waving toward the food, Attain stated, "No, no, of course not." Then he leaned forward and grabbed his glass of whiskey off the side table and held it up. With a wink, he claimed, "As long as you don't mind me drinking in front of you."

"Not at all," Ssimeas told him, a smile curving his wide lips. Then he reached for his plate and rested it on one thickly muscled thigh. "I understand you've had a number of shocks today, and I'm sorry I'm going to be adding to them." After that comment, Ssimeas picked up an egg, sausage, and cheese sandwich and took a big bite.

He just ate a third of that in one bite. Sexy!

Oh fuck. Did I just think that?

Attain cleared his throat, then took a deep swig of his whiskey. The liquid burned just right as it went down his throat. His stomach warmed as the alcohol settled there.

After swallowing a second gulp, Attain focused on Nicholas. "So, you've explained everything going on at the ranch and totally rocked my brain." He licked his lips, removing the last traces of the whiskey from them. "What else is there?" Then Attain held up his nearly empty tumbler. "And if it's heavy shit, I want more whiskey."

"Of course." Spieron popped out of his seat. With a wide grin and a flourish, he brandished the decanter of whiskey as he flashed his fangs. "From what I heard of your proclivities, you're going to need it for this."

Attain found his focus riveted to those ultra-sharp canines as Spieron topped up his tumbler. "Wow. Fangs. Vampires. Shifters." He shook his head, recalling how Nicholas had told him one of his ranch hands shared his spirit with a cougar. Frowning, Attain absently asked, "How come the cattle aren't afraid of the cat shifter?" Then he returned his focus to Ssimeas and waved his hand toward his huge, hulking, handsome frame. "Or you guys?"

Huge, hulking, handsome? Did I really just think that?

Attain knew he had. He just didn't understand why. He'd never looked twice at a male before.

"We're just another form of sentient being on the planet, Attain," Spieron told him, returning the decanter to the sideboard. "For the most part, as a prey animal, they don't see us different than humans. They consider us both predators and treat us accordingly."

"It's humans that think differently," Bodb pointed out. "With their racial prejudices and discrimination, we have to be careful who we share all this with." He glanced at Nicholas, resting his hand on his thigh possessively. "But my mate trusts you, so we told you everything." Then Bodb's eyes narrowed, and his focus shifted to Ssimeas. "Well, *almost* everything. There is *one* more important bit that you need to know."

"If it's that I need to promise never to tell a soul, I kinda figured that out on my own." Attain grinned as he waggled his brows. "No sense causing trouble with my practice by making wild accusations, right? My dad would—" Snapping his mouth shut, he felt his eyes widen as realization hit. "Shit!" Attain jumped to his feet as he yanked out his phone. Seven-ten. "I—" His phone vibrated in his hand, and he felt the blood drain from his face. "Fuck!"

"What's wrong?" All the other men in the room had risen to their feet. Ssimeas had put his sandwich down—or finished it, Attain wasn't certain—and hovered close. He had his clawed hands near to Attain's shoulders as if he wanted to touch and soothe him. "What's the matter?"

"I was supposed to be at my father's at six-thirty," Attain admitted as he hit accept on his phone. He held up his index finger, asking for silence. "Hey, Father. Sorry I'm not there."

"Me, too," George growled softly. "I'd ask if you were on your way, but it's too quiet for you to be in your *Avalanche*." From his tone, Attain knew his father was more than a little displeased. "Where are you?"

Attain closed his eyes and tipped his head back. "I'm at Nicholas's," he admitted. Thinking quickly, he added, "Something happened, and I—"

"What the fuck could have possibly happened so you couldn't meet your obligation?" George snarled, cutting him off. That, coupled with the cussing, told Attain exactly how pissed his father actually was. Before Attain could hope to figure out a suitable response, George spoke again, his tone cold and hard. "You have embarrassed me by standing up our dinner companions."

Frowning, Attain snapped open his eyes. "Dinner companions? What do you mean?" *What the hell?* "I thought we were meeting to discuss business."

"What you *thought* is beside the point," George rumbled gruffly. He cleared his throat. "How soon until you can get here?"

"Uh—" Attain stared at the glass of whiskey in his hand, so damn tempted to take a gulp. Even if he didn't, he knew he shouldn't be driving. "I—Well—"

To Attain's surprise, Ssimeas reached out and eased the phone from his hand. "Mister Walsh? This is Ssimeas, one of the ranch hands here. I'm sorry, but your son's in no condition to drive."

Attain gaped, shocked at Ssimeas's audacity.

Ssimeas just winked as he listened to whatever George said to him. "Well, sir, unfortunately there was a riding mishap, and he took a tumble." Waggling his brows, Ssimeas appeared completely unrepentant that he was spinning such lies. "Attain has a concussion, so we're keeping an eye on him this evening."

Glancing at Nicholas, Attain wondered what his buddy would have to say about Ssimeas's behavior. To his surprise, he saw his friend relaxing on the sofa, smirking. Even Bodb sported an amused smile.

"I was a medic in the military before choosing a slower pace of life and becoming a wrangler for Mister Lindson. That's how I know, sir."

Upon hearing that George continued to question Ssimeas, Attain realized his father wasn't going to let it go. He motioned for the phone back as he focused on Nicholas. "Can you loan me a nice shirt and drive me out there?"

"I can," Nicholas confirmed, nodding. "What's got your father in such a tizzy?"

Attain shook his head as he accepted the phone from Ssimeas. "Sorry, Father," he said to cut off George's rant about crack-pot medical people. There might have been something in there about suing Ssimeas if anything happened to Attain. "Nicholas will drive me out there, if you can add an extra plate to the dinner table."

"Certainly," his father stated, sounding happy now that he'd gotten his way. "And have him bring his lovely wife. I haven't seen either of them since the wedding."

Even as Attain relayed George's words to Nicholas, he wondered why his father would make such a comment. They never saw each other *before* the wedding, either.

Whatever.

"Uh, Sandra?" Nicholas turned his attention to his soon-to-be ex-wife, who was seated on another love seat curled up with her significant other, Maggie.

Attain had no idea when they'd joined them.

Sandra shrugged. "Sure. We haven't made an appearance together in a while, and our annulment hasn't come through, yet." Her expression appeared a little troubled as she focused on Maggie. "I can offer some guesses as to why my father hasn't shared the news with his friends, and I don't like it. Is it okay if Nicholas and I go together, babe?"

Maggie nodded. "It's fine, my familiar. It won't be for too much longer," she crooned, threading her fingers through Sandra's hair. Then, before she pecked a kiss to Sandra's lips,

Maggie murmured, "Don't be out too late."

"I won't," Sandra promised between pecking kisses.

"Thanks, Father. Set two plates," Attain stated into the phone, feeling his face warm as he stared at the floor so he didn't have to continue watching Sandra and Maggie exchanging loving words. While he didn't have a problem with same-sex couples, Attain had spent so many years associating Sandra with Nicholas, seeing her with another still caused his gut to churn with discomfort. "We'll be there as soon as possible."

Then Attain hung up his phone and shoved it into his pocket. When he felt a rough hand cradle his jaw, he jerked his gaze upward. He gaped in surprise as he finally noticed just how close to him Ssimeas stood.

And why is he touching me?

"You will come back this evening with them?"

While Ssimeas phrased it as a question, his tone made it sound more like a demand.

"Uh—" Attain tried to form words, but he found himself getting lost in the male's dark-gray eyes and his intense gaze.

"We'll bring him back," Nicholas assured, but Attain couldn't tear his focus from Ssimeas.

Feeling Ssimeas's thumb-claw slide under his lower lip, scraping ever-so-slightly, the hairs on Attain's neck stood on end and warmth trickled down his chest. His nipples beaded, and butterflies bounced around his belly. Even his cock swelled in his jeans.

What the fuck?

Attain swallowed hard, getting moisture into his suddenly too-dry throat. "Wh-Why?" he managed to croak out.

"Because of this."

Ssimeas's response made absolutely no sense to Attain. Except, then he dipped his head and sealed his mouth over Attain's own. Gasping in shock, he parted his lips.

The gargoyle took complete advantage.

In the next instant, Attain found himself with a mouthful of gargoyle tongue. He thought he should be grossed out . . . or maybe offended as the male took the liberty of mapping his mouth. The way he teased along Attain's own appendage, however, how he coaxed and lapped, caused a wash of fiery tendrils to burst through him.

Attain grabbed Ssimeas's upper arms and gave himself over to the kiss. Sagging against him, he obeyed when the male cradled his nape and used the hold to tilt his head. Vaguely, Attain recognized the pressure of Ssimeas's other hand on his hip, holding him close and steady.

Finally, Ssimeas broke the kiss.

Gasping for a new reason—because he desperately needed air in his lungs—Attain stared up at the gargoyle in shock.

Ssimeas smiled hungrily at him, his desire glimmering in eyes that had darkened to the color of thunderhead clouds.

Attain's brain finally caught up. "What the fuck did you do that for?" He realized he rested most of his weight against him. Pulling away, Attain felt his knees tremble a little. "What's going on?"

When had a kiss ever damn near knocked my socks off like that?

Nothing came to mind.

And my cock is throbbing. Shit!

"You are my mate, Attain," Ssimeas stated simply. Then he motioned toward one sofa, then another, conspicuously empty. "Just as Nicholas is Bodb's mate. And Albert is Spieron's mate." Then his thick eyebrow ridges furrowed as he amended, "Although, vampires call their mate a beloved."

"Wait a minute." Attain peeled his hands off the big male's arms and took a step backward, forcing the gargoyle to release him. "What the hell are you saying?"

"Now really isn't the time," Bodb stated as he opened the door, returning. "Nicholas has a shirt and jacket for you, Attain. When we return, we will explain in depth."

"Or we can in the truck," Nicholas offered, striding into the room, having already changed and carrying the aforementioned clothing. "But they're probably right." He held out the dress shirt. "Ditch that polo shirt, Attain."

Attain's mind reeled as he whipped his shirt over his head. *Just how long were we making out for?*

Taking the clothing, Attain pulled it on, then quickly did up the buttons. While Nicholas was a smidge broader than him, it still fit okay. Then Attain pulled on the jacket and buttoned that, too.

"Aww . . . I missed seeing your chest?" Sandra teased as she swept into the room, now wearing a sun-yellow cocktail dress that swished around her thighs. Somehow, she'd even swept her hair up into a French twist. Her blue eyes glimmered with mischief. "Guess I dressed too slow."

Maggie snorted as she followed Sandra. "You're not interested in anything he has anyway."

"True," Sandra agreed. She wrapped her arm around Maggie's waist and pressed a peck to her temple. "But that doesn't mean I can't admire it. You would, too, hon."

Sweeping an assessing, brown-eyed gaze over Attain's frame, Maggie hummed. "You're probably right."

"I've walked into an episode of *The Twilight Zone*," Attain muttered, shaking his head. "I-I think it's time to go."

"It is indeed," his best friend confirmed.

Nicholas gave Bodb a kiss while Sandra did the same to Maggie. To Attain's shock, Ssimeas once again reeled him in and laid one on him. This kiss was hard and felt possessive as all get-out. When Ssimeas released him, Attain stared up at him as he panted harshly.

"See you soon," Ssimeas stated.

At the same time, Attain asked, "Why do you keep doing that?"

"Come on, Attain," Nicholas called, drawing his attention. "All will be explained in time. Let's go deal with your father, first."

28

Attain nodded as he headed across the room. As he moved, he grabbed his tumbler of whiskey. Tipping it back, he drained the last of it. He handed the glass to Bodb as he passed him, then exited the family room.

He couldn't help glancing over his shoulder and getting one last glimpse of the sexy horned gargoyle.

Good god. Did I really just think that?

Attain shut down that line of thinking as he climbed into Nicholas's truck. As annoying as his father's insistence was, he appreciated the break from all things paranormal.

That shit is crazy.

Thirty minutes later, Attain walked into his father's large home and realized he would rather be back at Nicholas's, dealing with the crazy of the paranormal.

Waiting in the salon with a drink in hand and a predatory gleam in her blue eyes . . . was Chrissy Alderman.

Fuck!

CHAPTER FOUR

"Stop pacing," Elder Bodb ordered, although his tone held amusement. "You're making me dizzy."

Ssimeas scoffed, knowing how ridiculous that statement was for a gargoyle to make. They flew, for crying out loud. If winging through the air didn't make them dizzy, watching him pace the living room certainly wouldn't do it.

Still, Ssimeas crossed to the sideboard and poured himself a tumbler of bourbon. "Want a refresher?" he asked, indicating the glass of vodka his elder was drinking.

Bodb downed the last of what was in his glass, then held it up, grinning widely.

Taking that as a yes, Ssimeas crossed to him and grabbed the tumbler. He poured his old friend a refill, then turned. As he crossed back to Bodb, he saw him lowering his phone.

As Bodb took the refilled glass, he waved the device in his other hand. "Just received a text from Nicholas. They're on their way back."

"About bloody time," Ssimeas grumbled, glancing at the clock. It was well past ten-thirty.

"I'm going to spank that girl," Maggie commented absently where she was sitting on the opposite loveseat enjoying a glass of white wine. "I told her to be back by ten."

Bodb chuckled as Ssimeas flopped onto the sofa. Having found his mate that evening, then having him disappearing for a few hours due to a family obligation, the elder had given him the evening off. No way would he have been able to concentrate on his job. Instead, Lebone and Sindrid were splitting it into smaller chunks throughout the evening.

They'd both congratulated him. They'd also offered him advice, since they had met Attain a few times over the last couple of months.

Ssimeas chose the corner Attain had been sitting in, so he could turn his head and smell the cushions. Sighing deeply, he inhaled again, allowing the masculine scent of his mate to soothe him.

"I wonder if Attain is into spanking," Ssimeas commented absently, reveling in his human's delicious aroma. His fingers twitched. "Tie him to the bed and redden his hard ass. Gods, the way he filled out those jeans."

Between wallowing in Attain's scent and his thoughts, his prick began to thicken behind the fabric of his loincloth. He hummed as he palmed his dick.

"That's enough, big man," Maggie teased. "Get your head out of the gutter."

Clearing his throat, Ssimeas snapped open his eyes. He wasn't even certain when he'd closed them. Noticing Bodb's amused expression, he knew if his skin had been even reasonably fair, he would be blushing.

Good thing I have a nice medium-blue hide.

Bodb grinned broadly at him and waggled his brow ridges, since he'd returned to his true form. His purple hide appeared even darker up against the tan of the sofa. His slate-gray wings were draped around his shoulders, and he had one gray-clawed foot resting on his knee.

Ssimeas admired the male, mostly because regardless of what form he was in, any time Nicholas walked into the room, he was comfortable enough to flop into his arms.

I want a relationship like that.

Hearing Maggie speaking, Ssimeas once again pulled himself out of his thoughts. "And I hate to break it to you, but you need to slow your roll with Attain."

Slow my roll?

"What does that mean?" Ssimeas gave her a narrow-eyed stare as he took a sip of his bourbon . . . waiting.

Maggie gave him a narrow-eyed stare. "Sandra told you not to steamroll him, but the second he needs to deal with a family issue, you started to do just that."

Ssimeas opened his mouth to deny her statement, but he snapped it closed just as quickly. Thinking of his actions, he realized she was right. His need, his instinct, to care for his mate had overridden every other thought.

Dipping his chin, Ssimeas murmured, "Point taken."

Reaching over, Maggie patted his hand. "I'm a witch, so I understand some of your desires to care for the other half of your soul." Her smile turned commiserating. "Sitting back and watching Sandra date Nicholas was"—she sighed deeply—"difficult. Even when he agreed to be her beard." Maggie took a deep breath, then beamed a smile as she glanced between the two gargoyles. "But Fate ended up rewarding my patience, and now I get to hold her in my arms every night."

"And Sandra's name won't be attached to Nicholas's forever," Bodb reminded her. "While I don't know how long magick-users live, I imagine the magick you channel combined with your connection with Sandra, you'll be around for a couple of centuries." He grinned as he recalled, "You did say your grandmother is still alive and well at one-hundred-eighty-seven."

Maggie nodded. "My grandmother Lidia." Then her face turned a light shade of pink as she twisted her fingers together. "Um. She asked if she could come out and see us. I, uh . . . I think she wants to make certain I'm safe"—she lifted her hand and pointed back and forth between them—"with you all." Then Maggie flapped absently toward the ceiling. "And the vampires."

Ssimeas realized she indicated not only Spieron who was

sleeping overhead, but also Spieron's friend, Darian, who had arrived with his beloved just the week before—a human named Claude. The man's mind had been altered by a demon, giving him what amounted to flashbacks, causing him to think he needed to rescue prisoners-of-war.

Everyone at the ranch knew that if Claude became aggressive and began asking about prisoners, they were to refer to Darian as his contact and get him there as swiftly as possible.

So far, they'd only had one incident—learning that Claude needed to avoid the barn when their blacksmith was working on the horses.

The faint sound of a truck's engine caught Ssimeas's attention. Anticipation surged through him. His breath caught in his chest.

My mate is back.

"Relax, Ssimeas," Bodb ordered softly, his tone taking on a soothing quality. "Allow Attain to come to you."

Ssimeas nodded. "Right." He whispered the word before lifting his tumbler, only to find it empty. "Huh."

While uncertain when he'd drank all his bourbon, Ssimeas set the tumbler aside.

"I'll get you more." Maggie rose and grabbed his discarded glass. Her eyes twinkled as she crossed to the sideboard. "Then I'll meet my Sandra and take her upstairs while you get through the rest of your explanations." As Maggie handed Ssimeas his refilled glass, her expression sobered. "Don't forget to tell him about the pregnancy thing."

As Maggie left, presumably to meet Sandra at the door and tell them they were still in the family room, Ssimeas sat frozen in his seat. His mind whirled, and trepidation beat out his anticipation.

The pregnancy thing.

"Something just caused your anxiety to spike," Bodb commented, resting his forearms on his thighs as he leaned toward him. Concern darkened his brown eyes. "What is it?"

Ssimeas swallowed hard before admitting, "You know how most gargoyles start eating cinnamon when they meet their mate, rendering their sperm infertile?" After seeing Bodb nod, he admitted, "I'm part of the one percent of gargoyles where that doesn't work."

Bodb straightened, his brow ridges lifting. "Really?" He cocked his head as he swept his gaze over him, clearly assessing him. "Is that why you always bed males?"

"It is."

"Then how do you know?"

Rubbing his hand over the back of his neck, Ssimeas admitted, "About three and a half centuries ago, I took cinnamon, just like every other gargoyle, and I bedded the daughter of a fellow clutch-mate. Celia." He grimaced, shaking his head. "She became pregnant. Gods, was Zurcon ever pissed," he muttered, referring to the woman's gargoyle father. "But I was head enforcer, so there wasn't much he could do." Lifting his shoulder in a half-shrug, he continued, "I did my duty by her, caring for her through the pregnancy, and she bore me a daughter, Willow. We co-parented, even though we weren't actually a couple."

Bodb took a sip of his vodka as he waved his hand in a *go on* gesture.

Ssimeas shrugged, uncertain what else his elder wanted to know.

The purple gargoyle snorted. "Don't leave me in suspense. What happened?"

"Oh, well, Celia eventually met her mate in a lion shifter. She went to live with his pride." Ssimeas frowned, thinking back. "And my daughter met her mate in a gargoyle from another clutch. They're both happily mated, last I heard. I talk to Willow several times a year, and she keeps me abreast of how Celia is doing."

After a soft grunt of acknowledgment, Bodb commented,

"So after your daughter mated, you petitioned to become an elder enforcer."

Ssimeas nodded.

"Well, I wouldn't worry too much about it." Bodb grinned as he indicated the door, which was opening. "Just have Attain eat the cinnamon."

"I'm allergic," Attain stated, following Nicholas into the room. "Why would you want me to eat it anyway?"

"Oh, shit," Nicholas mumbled as he crossed the room to join Bodb on the love seat. "I totally forgot about that."

Feeling his gut clench, Ssimeas almost rose. He spotted the wary look in Attain's blue eyes as his human slowly crossed to the sofa. Ssimeas stayed his desire to pull his mate into his arms, to assure him that they would figure it out . . . mainly because he knew not only wouldn't his human understand, but he most likely wouldn't appreciate it.

Being so close to my mate and unable to touch him truly sucks great big donkey balls.

Win his trust first.

I can do this.

Except, then Attain sat down, and his scent wafted over Ssimeas's senses. He growled low in his throat upon catching the heavy overlay of perfume . . . and something decidedly feminine. Pinning a feral glare on Attain, Ssimeas rested his right hand on the sofa cushion between them and inhaled again.

"Who the fuck was hanging all over you like a spider monkey?" Ssimeas demanded.

Attain's eyes widened, and he leaned away from Ssimeas. "What?"

"You're drenched in some female's scent. Who were you with?"

"Ease back and relax, Ssimeas," Nicholas ordered, his tone firm. "It wasn't Attain's fault."

Ssimeas clenched his teeth as he obeyed the elder's mate.

Gripping his tumbler tightly, he scowled at the human. "Explain."

"We walked in the door and discovered George, that's Attain's father, had set up an ambush date." Nicholas grimaced while shaking his head. "Chrissy Alderman and her father were there. As soon as Attain arrived, Chrissy latched onto his arm and pressed her attributes against him, if you take my meaning."

A low growl escaped Ssimeas. He just couldn't help himself. The image of some random bimbo rubbing her tits all over his mate caused a coil of possessive anger to surge through him.

"You are *my* mate," Ssimeas grumbled, glaring at Attain. "No one should be touching you but me."

Attain scowled. "There's that word again. Mate." Then his brows shot up. "Oh, fuck, no! I've heard Bodb call Nicholas his mate." Pointing at Ssimeas, then at himself, Attain muttered, "You think *I'm* your mate? Like Nicholas is Bodb's mate?" He shook his head. "No."

Ssimeas felt his heart constrict in his chest upon hearing Attain's flat out denial. That simple word sent a wash of panic through him. He fought his urge to jump up, grab Attain, and whisk him away somewhere where they could be alone, and Ssimeas could spend hours, days, pleasuring and wooing his human.

"Calm down," Elder Bodb rumbled soothingly. "We warned you he'd have that knee-jerk reaction. Most humans do."

Nodding, Ssimeas took a sip of his drink while struggling to get his thoughts in order.

Fortunately, Nicholas took up the explanation. "A gargoyle doesn't just randomly pick someone and say, you're my mate." He patted Bodb's leg as he murmured, "How about some drinks. What do you want, Attain?"

"Maybe I shouldn't drink anything else," Attain muttered, rubbing his palm over his face. "I'm pretty damn sober at this point. I could just go home."

"Not, yet, my friend," Nicholas countered. "You need to understand this before you leave. It's important."

Bodb rose and crossed to the sideboard. "How about a beer to nurse, Attain?" As he made the offer, he pulled a pair of bottles from the mini-fridge.

"O-Okay."

Relief trickled through Ssimeas that Attain was at least willing to listen to his friend.

After Bodb had given Attain the drink and retaken his seat, Nicholas began again. "Okay, so. The first thing you need to know is a paranormal considers finding their mate the greatest gift Fate can give them."

"Fate?" Attain cocked his head as he cast a side-eyed gaze Ssimeas's way. "You believe in Fate?"

"We do," Ssimeas confirmed. "You would have felt attracted to me regardless." He spotted the slight flush to Attain's cheeks as he lowered his gaze to his beer. Needing to soothe his human's discomfort, Ssimeas reached over and touched his thigh. Smiling, he told him, "But Fate gives us that extra push to act on our desires when we otherwise might have walked away or resisted."

"You think I'm attracted to you?" Attain mumbled, glancing his way once more. "I've never been into a guy before, so why would you think that?"

Ssimeas eased closer on the sofa. Seeing Attain stiffen, he stopped when there was still several inches between them, even though he would much rather pull his reluctant human into his arms, so he could replace Chrissy's scent with his own. Rubbing Attain's thigh gently, Ssimeas gave him a smug smile.

"A gargoyle has a very keen sense of smell," Ssimeas told

him, eyeing the bulge behind Attain's fly. "That's how a gargoyle first recognizes who their mate is. By smell." Skimming his claws up the inseam of Attain's jeans, Ssimeas didn't miss the way his human sucked in a harsh gasp or how he instinctively spread his legs . . . just a little. "And I can smell your arousal, Attain," he crooned, leaning closer, allowing his hunger to drip from his voice. "I can smell how much I turn you on." Unable to help himself, Ssimeas added, "You make my cock throb with need, too, Attain. I would be so happy to bend over and let you mount me, driving us both to the greatest heights of pleasure."

Gaping, Attain whispered, "You'd let me top you?"

Ssimeas nodded once, slowly, while holding Attain's blue-eyed gaze. His human's nostrils were flared, and his desire had darkened his baby blues to a stormy color. Attain's need practically rolled off him, making Ssimeas salivate.

"I *need* you to mount me, handsome mate," Ssimeas admitted. "I need your seed flooding my channel."

"Need it?"

Loving the breathy sound of Attain's voice, Ssimeas felt a fresh surge of arousal spike through him. His cock throbbed, and pre-cum oozed from him. He bet if he looked down, he would see a wet spot forming on his loincloth.

Instead, Ssimeas held Attain's gaze and told him, "To forge our bond, we swap seed and blood, binding us for eternity." He massaged Attain's muscular thigh and added, "I will be yours, and you will be mine. Mine to keep safe, to care for, to pleasure."

In hindsight, Ssimeas realized he'd said exactly the wrong thing.

Attain leaped to his feet, pulling from his grip. "I gotta go," he mumbled, glancing around the room wildly.

"Attain, wait—" Nicholas called, but Attain didn't.

Instead, Attain waved as he hustled from the room, calling,

"I'll talk to you later. Don't worry. I won't tell." Then he was out the sliding door and out of sight.

Ssimeas rose, intending to follow and bring him back.

"Let him go," Nicholas advised. When Ssimeas paused and turned back to him, the human told him, "He's had a shit-ton of stuff dumped on him today. Give him a day or two to process." Then Nicholas grinned and offered him an eyebrow waggle. "Then I'll help you start wooing him like a human." His expression grew serious again. "I've felt the mate-pull, so I know what he'll be feeling. He may fight it for a little while, but he'll get over it. Trust me."

Flopping back onto the sofa, Ssimeas nodded. He heard the roar of an engine, telling him Attain was tearing down the driveway.

I sure hope Nicholas is right because I don't really have much of a choice.

CHAPTER FIVE

Attain had expected Nicholas to drop by his condo on Sunday . . . but he hadn't. Instead, he'd received a text from his friend — a single line.

Tell me you're doing okay.

Staring at the few words, Attain had immediately typed — *Yeah, sure.* Then he'd erased it because it hadn't been true. After fifteen minutes of staring at his phone, he'd replied — *I'm processing.*

Ten minutes later, Attain received a short response.

If you have any questions, just ask.

Attain didn't even know where to begin, so he replied simply — *I will.*

That had been it.

For the rest of the afternoon and evening, Attain had worked in his home office and caught up on files. He'd buried himself in work. Still, it had been damn difficult to focus.

Every time Attain allowed his mind to stray, his thoughts drifted to a certain big, blue gargoyle. Rubbing his face, he closed his eyes. His memory immediately conjured up an image of Ssimeas.

Attain felt his blood heat and head south. Groaning, he leaned back in his comfortable office chair. He spread his legs and sighed deeply, enjoying the sensation of arousal.

He'd always loved sex . . . and he'd had it often. Going into a bar and picking up a bimbo for the evening had never been a hardship. Thinking back, he recalled the last woman he'd been with — a slightly plump, big-boobed brunette with wavy curls.

Sighing, Attain lifted his hips and shoved down his sweatpants. His cock bobbed out, twitching and jerking. He gripped himself with his right hand while cupping his balls with his left.

Moaning softly as he jacked himself, Attain recalled her smooth, soft skin. He thought of how he'd sprawled on the hotel room bed, allowing him to watch her breasts bounce as she'd ridden him. Her big nipples had been beaded and swollen from his sucking, and they'd gleamed beautifully in the dim moonlight coming through the room's window.

As Attain remembered the feel of her sheath milking him, his erection began to wane. Instead of drawing closer to his release, he softened. He clenched his teeth and sped up his strokes while thinking of how her dark hair had brushed over his chest.

"Damn it," Attain grumbled, snapping his eyes open. "What the hell did that gargoyle do to me?"

Thinking of Ssimeas, just that fast, Attain's dick began to plump anew. He thought of the feel of his swarthy skin, wondering if it felt like that everywhere. The male's huge black wings called for him to rub his erection over them.

Would they be silky soft? Or leathery like his hide?

Attain moaned as he felt his hard cock twitch in his grip. His pre-cum oozed from his slit, creating a delicious tingle as it dripped down his crown. He stared down at himself as he teased at his balls . . . then further back.

When Attain rubbed the tip of his pinky lightly over his puckered entrance, he sighed roughly. He did it again, and his gut clenched. When he dipped the tip of his finger into himself, Attain moaned roughly.

The image of Ssimeas's claw-tipped digit easing into his body popped into his head, and he closed his eyes as his breath caught in his throat. His anus had always been sensitive, and he fingered himself often. Ssimeas's digits were bigger and tipped with lethal-looking claws.

What would it feel like to have Ssimeas do this to him, to have his thick finger pushed into his chute? Would he gently scrape his claw along his inner lining?

Attain groaned roughly, a tremble working through him. His cock throbbed, and his balls rolled. Pushing his finger in deeper, Attain sought out his prostate, imagining it was Ssimeas's claw sliding across his gland.

As a spark of pleasure burst through him from the inside out, Attain jolted in his chair. Heat erupted through his groin. His orgasm crashed through him as shudders racked his body.

Somehow, spots managed to flash across the backs of his eyelids as shivers rolled through him. He panted harshly as he rested his head against the back of the chair. Reveling in the sensations created by his release, he gently pulled his finger from his chute, letting out a deep sigh in the process.

For several moments, Attain just floated on the blissful endorphins pinging through his system.

Then the image of Ssimeas's smug, toothy smile flashed through his mind's eye.

Attain sighed again as he recalled the gargoyle's image. His curved black horns begged for his touch. He wanted to explore the creature's wide shoulders, heavily muscled frame, and his eight-pack abdominals.

So fucking sexy.

Releasing his genitals, Attain peered down at his still half-hard dick. He thought about Ssimeas's tail, and he wondered if he could use it like a handle as he powered into the gargoyle's ass. His prick twitched, liking the direction of his thoughts, and Attain groaned.

Shaking his head, Attain kicked off his sweats. He pushed to his feet and padded barefoot and naked to his bedroom's ensuite. After turning on the water and adjusting it to the temperature he wanted, Attain stepped inside.

Attain rested his forearms on the tile walls and bowed his head, placing his forehead on the right one.

What the hell am I going to do?

Sitting behind his desk at the office come Monday morning, Attain did his best to keep his head on work . . . instead of the epic orgasm he'd gotten just from imagining Ssimeas fingering him . . . or the second one he'd had in the shower, imagining the water flowing over him was actually the gargoyle's wings caressing his skin.

Goddammit! Focus!

Attain scowled at his screen and forced his attention back to the document he was reviewing. For the next couple of hours, he managed to get some work done. He had just hit save when the tap of someone knocking on his door caught his attention.

"Enter," Attain called as he opened his email program. He felt his brows shoot up his forehead as he watched his receptionist, Priscilla, enter carrying a big bouquet of red roses in a large purple vase with a yellow ribbon tied in a bow around it. "Prissy? What's that?"

As soon as the words were out of his mouth, Attain wanted to roll his eyes.

Duh!

Prissy giggled, a wide smile curving her lips. "Well, I *think* it's a dozen red roses." She set them on his desk and rested her hands on her hips, looking pleased as all get-out.

"And why are you bringing them to me?" Attain asked even as he leaned forward and sniffed one of the fragrant buds.

"Because it's addressed to you," Prissy told him. She pointed at the envelope tucked between the tines of the plastic stick sunk into the dirt. "It has your name on it."

Attain gripped the vase and turned it, giving him a better look at the envelope. "Huh. So it does." It did, too. In a scrolling cursive, someone had written his name.

"Come on," Prissy urged. "Who's it from?" Another giggle erupted from her. "Are you actually dating someone, Mister Confirmed Bachelor?" Then Prissy pressed her hands over her breasts. "Is it that girl from the wedding?"

"No," Attain quickly replied, shaking his head. No way did he want that rumor going around. As Attain eased the envelope from the holder, he added, "Besides, Chrissy is the kind of girl who'd expect *me* to send *her* flowers."

After easing the card from the envelope, Attain read the words. His lips parted, betraying his surprise, before he could help himself. His blood heated and flowed south . . . and even a little into his cheeks.

Holy shit! No way am I blushing.

Except, as Attain cleared his throat and began putting the card back into the envelope, he knew he was.

"Oh, no you don't," Prissy cried, snatching the card from his fingers.

Knowing that trying to grab it back would only make it worse, Attain swallowed to get moisture into his throat as he watched Prissy read the words on the card.

My handsome Attain — I can't stop thinking about the time we spent together Saturday. The memory of your skin beneath my hands still causes my palms to tingle. Looking forward to hearing your voice and seeing you again gives me reason to rise each day. Thinking of you — Ssimeas.

"Ohhhh! That's the sweetest thing I've ever read." Prissy let out a deep sigh as she placed her hand over her chest, still staring at the card. "Who's Ssimeas? Where did you meet her?"

Attain cleared his throat and shifted restlessly in his seat. How could he explain this? Then he recalled Ssimeas's comments on the phone to his father, and he realized the gargoyle had already given him the perfect cover story.

"Ssimeas is a man. He's a wrangler out at Nicholas's ranch."

Prissy gaped, her eyes going wide. A second later, she gasped, "I didn't know you were gay." Then Prissy's cheeks took on a pinkish hue. "I-I mean, um, I always saw you with women. Are you bisexual?" Her face grew even darker, the color spreading down her neck. "I'm so sorry, Attain. Sir. Um . . . that's none of my business."

Unable to help himself, Attain chuckled softly. He couldn't remember the last time he'd seen Prissy so flustered. On top of that, he couldn't muster up any offense at being asked if he was gay or bisexual.

Attain had always thought what people did in their bedroom with someone they cared about was their own damn business.

"It wasn't like that," Attain still countered as he grinned broadly. "The horse I was riding slipped and fell in some mud, taking me with it. I hit my head on a rock. Ended up with a mild concussion." Shrugging, Attain told her, "Ssimeas used to be a medic in the military, and he helped me out." Turning his attention to the roses, he reached out and skimmed his fingertips along the edge of one of the large red blooms. He recalled the kiss he'd shared with him, and his blood heated in his veins. "But damn, the man can kiss."

Hearing Prissy make a strangled noise somewhere between a laugh, a snort, and a snicker, Attain yanked his hand away, realizing what he'd blurted out. He cleared his throat as he held up his hand. "The card, please."

Prissy smirked as she handed it back. "So, you kissed the man while concussed. Huh." While her cheeks still retained just a smidge of pink, she'd returned to her usual playful confidence. "Are you going to see him again?"

"Uh . . ." Attain rubbed the back of his neck. Was he going

to see him again? "Well, he works for Nicholas, so —"

Except, if he always went during the day, Ssimeas would always be asleep roosting . . . not that he could say that. Oddly enough, that thought caused his gut to twist.

Why?

Because of that mate shit?

"So, you have an admirer at Nicholas's ranch." Prissy continued to smile as she touched the roses. "A bouquet like this is costly, Attain. Must have taken quite a chunk out of a cowhand's salary. He must really, really like you."

Attain rubbed at his chest, knowing the truth of those words. "I guess so."

I may need to find out a bit more about this mate business.

"You have a call waiting on line three, Attain," George stated, striding into his office. "It came in to my receptionist since Priscilla didn't pick up. What's going on?" Then George's attention fell to the bouquet of roses. "Oh, are you going to give those to Chrissy?"

Priscilla offered Attain a small smile, saying, "I'll get information on that call." When she turned, she dipped her head at George. "Sir."

Seeing no way out of revealing the truth, Attain shook his head. "No, actually. These were sent to me by Ssimeas."

"Ssimeas? Who is —" George paused, his eyes narrowing. A muscle ticked in his jaw. "You mean that *medic* from Nicholas's place?"

Attain nodded. "The very same."

He kept a straight face even though he wanted to scowl. For some reason, the way his father said *medic*, as if it was a dirty word, caused irritation to surge through him. He vaguely wondered what the man would think if he knew Ssimeas wasn't actually a medic but a gargoyle.

And I can never tell him . . . and he can never find out either.

A sneer curving his lips, George grumbled, "I had no idea Nicholas employed *their* kind."

Well, damn.

"Didn't realize you were homophobic." The words were out of Attain's mouth before he could think better of them. Upon seeing George's cheeks darken and his brown eyes narrow, he quickly added, "I don't much care what other people do in their bedroom."

George stabbed a finger in the direction of the roses. "Except now he wants to bugger you. That doesn't bother you?"

"Kinda flattering, actually."

God, where is this shit coming from? Why can't I control my mouth?

Seeing George's face darken further, Attain quickly continued with a laugh, "Come on. It's nice to know you attract attention." Then he peered toward the door, seeing Prissy appear with an expectant look on her face. "Anyway," he hurriedly continued. "Thanks for letting me know about that call. It looks like Prissy has it ready for me."

George's sneer remained as he turned and started toward the door. Shaking his head, he stalked from the room. He muttered under his breath as he left.

Attain fought back a cringe as he made out his father's words. "At least with you dating Chrissy, no one will get the wrong idea."

Shaking his head, Attain did his best to ignore Prissy's questioning look as he asked her, "Who's on the line?"

CHAPTER SIX

"You have to stop sending me stuff at work."

Reclining on the hay bale, Ssimeas smirked at the barn ceiling. He'd woken from roost five minutes before and discovered a missed call on his cell phone. His heart had just about pounded out of his chest when he'd realized it was from Attain.

It seemed Nicholas's advice to send wooing gifts to Attain at his work was paying off. Even though his mate was calling to request he stop, he was still calling. Ssimeas would be happy with any contact at all.

"Why, my mate?" Ssimeas asked softly, his deep voice still a little rough from sleep. Scratching at his abdominals absently, he continued, "Did you not enjoy the gifts?"

On Monday, Ssimeas had had a large bouquet of red roses delivered to his human. He'd made certain gifts were sent to Attain each day that week—chocolates, a cookie bouquet, and a fruit basket, respectively. Those were nothing compared to what he had planned for the following afternoon.

Ssimeas grinned, wishing he could be there to see Attain's face when the singing telegram arrived. He hadn't even realized that was a thing. Nicholas had found the company, assuring him it would make a statement.

"What statement is that?" Ssimeas had asked, confused.

What does a singing, dancing man in a cowboy outfit say?

With a grin, Nicholas had replied, "That you're a fun guy with a sense of humor that just wants to make your man smile."

Ssimeas had just nodded, uncertain how to respond.

"If I ate that many sweets each week, I wouldn't be able to fit in my suits within a month."

Attain's melodious tenor drew Ssimeas back to where it should be—his mate. Unable to help himself, he quickly responded, "I would be more than happy to help you work off all those calories." Just the thought of calisthenics with Attain caused his dick to thicken behind his loincloth.

Cupping himself, Ssimeas rubbed lightly, humming appreciatively at the stimulation.

A strangled sort of groan came through the line before Attain asked, "Are you . . . are you, um . . . t-touching—" His voice squeaked a little, and he snapped his jaw shut so loudly Ssimeas could hear it through the line.

Hmm. Someone likes that idea.

"I am," Ssimeas answered honestly. "Your voice is sexy, and thinking of sharing sweaty, physical activity with you—" Ssimeas groaned huskily, expressing his need without words.

"Shit," Attain muttered, his voice deepening and betraying his growing arousal. "God, you're—" He paused and cleared his throat. "Look. Sure, I enjoyed the gifts, but they're disrupting the office. Why didn't you send them to my house?"

"I didn't send them to your house because Nicholas said you're a work-a-holic and are rarely ever home," Ssimeas admitted, doing his best to be honest with his mate. "And by sending them to your office, I am announcing my pursuit of you. I'm showing any other would-be suitors that they have stiff competition."

"Nicholas is helping you pick out things?"

"He is," Ssimeas confirmed. Then he remembered Attain's other comment. "You getting gifts at work is disrupting your office?" Ssimeas repeated, trying to understand. He slid his hand off his dick and rested it on his abdominals, tapping his forefinger restlessly. "How so?"

As much as Ssimeas wanted to remain at the forefront of Attain's mind every day, he didn't want to cause problems.

Attain heaved a sigh before telling him, "Well, everyone comes by to see if I got something new, and my father—" He groaned, the sound one of frustration.

"Is it because I'm a guy?" Ssimeas hazarded a guess.

"Yes and no," Attain answered slowly.

Ssimeas rolled his eyes. "Which is it, my mate? I can't help if I don't know."

"People keep stopping by my office to see what you sent. They give me shit and ask how long we've been dating, when I'm going to bring you to the office so they can meet you, and when I'm going to tie the knot." Attain's words were rushed, and his tone was filled with frustration. "My father was furious the first time he heard that question, and now he's announcing that I'm dating Chrissy and we're in a serious relationship any time someone asks about the gifts and—Fuck!"

Possessive rage surged through Ssimeas, but he beat it back with the knowledge that his antics had caused his mate discomfort.

"I didn't mean to cause you stress, my mate," Ssimeas rumbled softly, searching for the right words to soothe his human. "It is too late to cancel the gift I have scheduled for you for tomorrow, but I vow not to—" Ssimeas paused, realizing he couldn't figure out how to finish his sentence.

After all, Ssimeas couldn't promise not to continue sending Attain gifts.

"Why are you sending me gifts at work, Ssimeas?" Attain asked quietly after a moment of silence. "You know I don't want a relationship." While Ssimeas swallowed hard, trying to get the lump in his throat to go down upon hearing Attain's rejection, his human added, "Look. I don't mean to hurt your feelings, but I tried the relationship route once, and it's not something I want to do again . . . even if you were a woman, which would have made the whole thing so much easier. Hell, now I have my father breathing down my neck about Chrissy, and even if I wanted to find a wife, she sure as hell wouldn't be someone I'd be interested in."

Once again, Attain had begun rambling, and Ssimeas found the information interesting, even as he gritted his teeth to keep from once again declaring that Attain was his and no other would touch him.

"Chrissy is a skinny, social-climbing trollop. I like my women bigger, so if I get enthusiastic, I don't have to worry about hurting her." Scoffing, Attain continued, "And more down-to-earth and someone who enjoys outside activities, so we have something to talk about and something to do together. I mean—"

"Attain," Ssimeas cut in, a growl in his voice, no longer able to continue listening to Attain's description of what had to have been his past conquests. "You need to stop."

"Huh?"

Ssimeas let out a low growl upon hearing Attain's confusion. "I don't know how many times I need to remind you of this," he ground out between clenched teeth. "Paranormals are possessive when they find the other half of their soul. You talking about your past like that . . . it's pissing me off."

"Uhhh—"

Managing to unclench his jaw, Ssimeas continued in a husky whisper, "Do you have any idea how badly I want to hunt you down and whisk you away from there?" He fought against the urge every evening. "I would take you to someplace secluded and lay you down on a bed of soft grass underneath the stars." His cock, which had softened listening to Attain's ramblings, began to harden again. "I would strip you of your clothes and lick every inch of your body."

Hearing Attain sucking in a surprised gasp, Ssimeas smiled. He licked his lips, wishing he was there to capitalize on Attain's parted lips. For the last four evenings, he had jacked off to his memory of Attain's kiss, and he desperately wanted to enjoy his mate's taste once more.

"I would suck your cock and drink your seed." Ssimeas's mouth watered at his own imaginings, and his eyelids slid shut. "Are you bitter, my mate? Or salty? Maybe salty-sweet?" He couldn't stop himself from moaning. "Gods, I want to find out so badly."

"Y-You do?" Attain rasped. "You would, you would suck my dick?"

"Oh, gods, yes, Attain. Happily. Hungrily." Ssimeas pressed the heel of his palm against the base of his erection. "I would lick you like a lollipop as I massaged your balls. Are yours sensitive?"

"Yes," Attain replied, his voice practically a squeak.

Ssimeas hummed, appreciating the honest reply. "Excellent," he purred. "I'll bathe them with my tongue while I tease your star with my finger. I know I have claws, but I'll be gentle. You have nothing to fear."

"Like playing with my ass. I-Imagined your claws in my chute, teasing my prostate," Attain mumbled around a groan. "Wondered what it would feel like. I—I can't believe I admitted that."

Grinning, Ssimeas untied the strings of his loincloth. "Have you now?" He didn't wait for an answer. Gripping his erection, Ssimeas gave himself a leisurely stroke. He heard his mate's breathy grunts and huffs, and an idea formed. "Do you have your dick out, Attain?" Ssimeas heard Attain's hum of assent and grinned broadly. "Me, too. Are you imagining what I'm doing to you?"

"Y-Yes."

The sound of Attain's strained voice caused a fresh spear of arousal to course through Ssimeas's body. His cock throbbed in his grip, and his balls felt heavy, swollen with his cum. He needed relief in the worst way and tightened his grip.

"I'll slide my finger into my mouth, getting it nice and wet, before pushing it deep into your body. I'll move my mouth to your cock and swallow you to the root." Ssimeas felt a surge of smug satisfaction as he heard Attain's breathy groan. "I will suck you so good, my mate, while teasing your prostate. Your body will stretch, craving the feel of me in you and on you. When I push a second finger into your chute, massaging your inner muscles so good, I'll tease at your frenulum while rolling your balls with my other hand."

Attain roared through the line, his enjoyment clear. He mumbled something too soft for even Ssimeas to make out. Then a whimpering hiss followed.

Ssimeas reveled in the sounds of Attain's enjoyment. His heart thudded with pride that he'd pleased his mate, even though he hadn't even touched him. Continuing to listen to Attain's raspy breathing, he gave his cock one more hard tug, and that was all he needed.

Growling Attain's name softly, Ssimeas sprayed his cum all over his chest. His hard pulses sent wave after wave of blissful endorphins coursing through his body. He panted harshly as he slowed his strokes, teasing the last bits of cum from his balls.

"H-Holy shit," Attain mumbled, his voice sounding raspy, perhaps from his shouts. "Can't believe I did that."

Knowing he sported a goofy, languid smile, Ssimeas stared at the barn's ceiling. "We are compatible, Attain," he stated huskily. "Admit it."

"Yeah. We are." Attain sighed deeply. "And I never said we aren't."

Ssimeas hummed. "True." As his mind began to come back online after such an epic release—*and, gods, just from talking my mate into orgasm and hearing his cries*—he began to process

Attain's earlier ramblings. Something clicked, and Ssimeas couldn't help but grin. "You know, I fulfill all those requirements you listed."

"Huh?"

Chuckling softly, Ssimeas told him, "You said if you were to date, it would be someone bigger, who could handle enthusiastic love-making. I am bigger and could easily handle any exuberance you may want to enjoy."

"Uh . . ."

Ssimeas didn't bother waiting for Attain to try to come up with a response. Instead, he pointed out, "And you mentioned how you wanted to be with someone who enjoyed outside activities, so you would have something to talk about and something to do together." Humming gruffly, Ssimeas claimed, "Also, me. I love being outdoors, and once we've bonded, I would be more than happy to explore everything with you."

"And the being able to carry on a conversation?" Attain asked slowly, his voice carrying an almost leery, disbelieving tone.

Grinning, Ssimeas glanced at his phone. "We have been chatting for over thirty minutes without issue, Attain."

"That doesn't mean it would continue," Attain countered.

"I believe it would," Ssimeas insisted. "After all, you are my mate, the man who holds the other half of my soul." When Attain didn't answer right away, Ssimeas added, "She is never wrong, even though we will have to work at it, just like any other couple."

Attain's sigh came through the line, loud and clear. "I don't know, Ssimeas."

Huh. That wasn't a no.

Ssimeas opened his mouth, ready to offer more encouragement, when Attain started talking again.

"I told you. I tried the relationship thing once, and I don't want to feel that kind of betrayal again." Attain's voice lowered, his uneasiness clearly bleeding through. "Sure, it starts out fine, but someone always winds up hurt when you get tired of each other. Instead of just explaining that, she—" Growling softly, Attain rumbled, "I don't want to talk about this."

Taking an educated guess from Attain's comments, Ssimeas asked softly, "Someone cheated on you, and it hurt, right?"

Attain snapped, "I told you I didn't want to talk about this." With another growl, he continued, "I can't believe Nicholas could hitch his wagon to Bodb after only knowing him for a few months. Who does that?"

"I would never cheat on you, Attain," Ssimeas assured, trying to draw the conversation back to them. "I promise you that."

"You can't make a promise like that," Attain claimed, sounding annoyed. "Who's to say how you'll feel ten years down the road or five years down the road, or hell, maybe you'll change your mind about this mating business in a month." He scoffed, the sound one of derision. "Just because I smell good now doesn't mean you'll always think so."

"Yes, it will," Ssimeas snapped, scowling at the ceiling. His heart hurt from the pain filling Attain's tone. Someone had hurt his mate . . . deeply.

"You can't—"

"Yes, I can," Ssimeas cut in. "I *can* say that, because that's how it works with paranormals." Suddenly recalling a particular fact about paranormals, he grinned. "Attain, once we bond, I won't even have the ability to get an erection for anyone else." Upon hearing the silence coming through the line, Ssimeas could just imagine Attain's shocked expression. "Once we bond, you will be it for me, my mate." Then he growled low in his throat as he added, "Just as *I* will be it for *you*. If another touches you, I will end them."

CHAPTER SEVEN

"Is what Ssimeas told me true?" Attain demanded softly, staring at Nicholas and Bodb.

Very similar to the Saturday before, Attain sat at his friend's dining room table early in the morning. He had driven his *Ducati* that time, however, since he'd been on the thing since just before sunrise. Attain had needed the hour and a half ride driving the back roads to decide if he was really going to drop by the ranch again.

In the end, Attain's curiosity had won out.

Bodb nodded once. "Yes, it's true. Once a paranormal bonds with his fated mate, he or she will not become aroused by another." Lifting his hand, he added, "That's not to say you won't have arguments, disagreements, or other issues, but cheating will never be one of them." Then Bodb growled softly, warning, "Well, not for the paranormal. If you were to ever attempt to be intimate with another, the decision would put that person's life in grave danger."

Attain nodded once. "I would never," he muttered, rotating the cup of coffee he cradled between his palms. His cheeks felt hot as he added, "I've been on the receiving end of that and—" Attain paused and shook his head.

Nicholas patted Bodb's wrist. "Attain comes across his commitment shyness honestly." Wincing, he added, "I hope you can get over it, man, because if you hold out for long, you're gonna start to get real uncomfortable."

Cocking his head and narrowing his eyes, Attain asked warily, "What do you mean?"

Bodb sighed deeply as he shrugged one shoulder. "Fate likes to get her way. Now that you've met, you're gonna have trouble getting it up for someone else, too."

"What?" Attain roared, leaping to his feet. Resting his knuckles on the table, he leaned toward his friend and his . . . male. "Are you saying I'm going to have trouble getting an erection, too?" Even as Attain barked out the question, he recalled how the only time he'd been able to jack off was when he was thinking about Ssimeas. "Shit."

"Already starting?" Nicholas commented, shaking his head with a sad smile. "Yeah, Fate is a bitch who likes to get her way." Then his eyes narrowed, and he waggled his eyebrows. "However, the amount of sex you will enjoy and the quality of it will be beyond anything you could ever get with another."

Recalling how hard he'd blown from just hearing Ssimeas's whispered and sensual words, a shudder worked through him.

Attain slowly lowered back to his seat. He grabbed his coffee and took a swig. While rubbing the back of his neck, he met Nicholas's gaze and nodded.

"Want a word of advice?" Nicholas asked softly, holding his gaze with an understanding expression.

Waving his hand in a *go ahead* motion, Attain shrugged.

Nicholas reached over and gripped Attain's hand. "Don't fight this. Give in." He squeezed, then released him, so he could thread his fingers with Bodb's. While smiling at his lover, Nicholas murmured, "It's worth it."

"This will turn my life upside down, Nick," Attain whispered, redrawing his friend's attention. Even as goose bumps worked down his spine, he swallowed hard. "My father is pushing me to marry because of you and Sandra."

Grimacing, Nicholas shook his head. "I'm sorry I was the catalyst."

"We should have just admitted we were in the process of getting an annulment when we had dinner over there last weekend," Sandra said, announcing her presence. "Can I get you a plate, hon?" As she spoke, she glanced over her shoulder, indicating that she spoke to Maggie, who trailed behind her.

"Thanks." Maggie pecked a kiss to Sandra's lips. "I'll get the coffee."

"Mmmm, yum," Sandra purred, then turned and started around the table toward the sideboard holding the breakfast items. She squeezed Attain's shoulder as she passed. "Morning, Attain. Back again, I see." Winking, Sandra added, "And Nicholas is right. It's totally worth it to bond with your paranormal. No matter the cost."

"Paranormal?" Vernon's confused voice caused everyone to whip their attention to the entranceway. Nicholas's brother glanced around the room with furrowed brows. "What are you guys talking about?"

"Oh, dear," Sandra whispered. Her gaze drifted between Maggie, Bodb, and Nicholas. "I—" Lowering her voice, Sandra mumbled, "Sorry."

Attain glanced around as he lifted his brows. "Vernon doesn't know?"

"Know what?" Vernon asked warily. He adjusted his glasses on his nose before crossing his arms over his chest. "What's going on?"

Heaving a sigh, Attain turned his attention back to his coffee. "Welcome to the rabbit hole, Vernon," he muttered after taking a sip. Then he rose to his feet, taking his mug with him. "I'm gonna go muck stalls."

"Stress relief, huh?" Nicholas commented knowingly. Pointing at the coffee station, he recommended, "You oughta take a travel mug to go."

Attain grunted, then finished his last couple swigs of coffee. After placing the dirty mug in a plastic tub that he knew Pauline—Nicholas's cook who he'd learned was a fox shifter—*crazy*—used to return the dishes to the kitchen, he headed to the coffee station. The counter had two carafes of coffee, each a different flavor, then one of standard decaf. There was also a carafe of hot water, which could be used with the various flavors of tea as well as the hot cocoa.

Nicholas certainly changed things up to accommodate his wealthy lover.

After making himself a paper *to go* cup of coffee, Attain headed out the door. He took a second to glance over his shoulder and spotted Nicholas urging Vernon to sit at the table. Sandra was sitting next to Maggie while Bodb was making up a plate of food for Nicholas's brother.

They're in for a long chat.

As Attain headed to the barn, he wondered how they'd managed to keep the secret of paranormals from Vernon for so long, seeing as the man had been living there for a couple of weeks. When he'd asked Nicholas about why his brother was living there, his best friend had explained it had to do with the family scandal. When Baltus, Nicholas's father, had been injured when he came off a horse and ended up in a coma, Nicholas had sought out the man he thought to be his uncle—Albert, Baltus's younger brother. Low and behold, once Albert returned home with a male lover at his side, Katrina—Nicholas's mother and Baltus's wife—had gone off the rails.

Attain thought it was the whole, be wary of a woman scorned thing, since it came out that Katrina had had an affair with Albert when they were young, and Nicholas was the result of that union. Katrina had forged paperwork and convinced Vernon that due to him being Baltus's true firstborn, the ranch was supposed to pass to him. Somehow, Albert and his lover, Spieron, had tricked Katrina into revealing the truth . . . and they'd made a recording of it.

Katrina had landed in jail, Vernon had dropped the proceeding to take the ranch from Nicholas, and Vernon had moved in with Nicholas until the hullabaloo in town died down.

It hadn't, yet.

Attain had been just as shocked as everyone else, but now he knew that some of what was public knowledge were lies. Paranormals had covered up their help in the matter. As it turned out, Spieron was a vampire, and he'd manipulated the minds of both Baltus and Katrina.

Shaking his head as Attain reached the barn, he inhaled deeply. He enjoyed the fragrance of horse, leather, cleaner, and hay, although he couldn't imagine having to deal with the responsibilities of caring for them every day. Just the idea of children scared the shit out of him.

Safe sex had been his best friend.

Attain crossed to the storage room where the cleaning supplies were kept and, after putting his half-finished coffee on a shelf, grabbed what he needed and got to work.

The mind-numbing simplicity of raking, scooping, and pushing and dumping a wheelbarrow helped ease Attain's stress. He cleaned one stall, then a second. While he was working on the third, he felt the hairs on the nape of his neck stand on end.

Turning, Attain found Spieron standing there. The auburn-haired vampire leaned against the stall wall, watching him. The man stared at him with piercing green eyes.

"Uh, Spieron?" Attain asked uncertainly. "Something you need?"

"Just checking to see if you're freaking out." The corners of Spieron's lips curved into a slight smile. "I have seen many humans brought into the fold, and often times, it can be difficult for your race to wrap your minds around the paranormal."

Attain leaned his rake against the wall and rested his hands on his hips. "It's not the paranormal that I'm struggling with," he admitted, shaking his head.

Arching his left brow, Spieron pressed, "Oh? Then what?" Then he grinned widely, a knowing expression crossing his lean features. "The man on man action thing? The pregnancy thing? Or the living for centuries with one partner thing?"

"I—" Attain scowled, his heart beginning to hammer in his chest. "What pregnancy thing?"

Spieron's mirth left his green eyes as he cocked his head. "The fact that gargoyles can get their male mates pregnant."

"What?" Attain gasped, stumbling a step backward.

"Oh, fuck. You didn't know?" Spieron grimaced as he lifted his hands, palms out. "I would have thought that would be one of the first things shared. It's an ability only gargoyles have . . . I think."

"Wh-What the hell are you talking about?"

Attain heard the squeak in his voice, but he couldn't seem to help himself. His heart pounded in his chest, and he suddenly felt short of breath. He stumbled, his back hitting the stall wall behind him, and he pressed his hand to his chest.

"Easy now," Spieron encouraged, suddenly standing directly in front of him. He rested his hand on Attain's shoulders and pressed downward. "Bend forward. Head between your knees. Take slow, deep breaths. Everything will be fine."

Obeying the vampire's urging, Attain rested his ass against the stall wall and bent over. He gripped his knees in a tight hold as he hung his head between them. Staring at the shavings-covered floor, he did his best to focus on the in and out action of his lungs.

"That's the way," Spieron encouraged, massaging his nape

lightly. "Now I see you're freaking out, but it really isn't necessary." As he reassured him, his tone turned soothing. "After all, there's an easy fix. All you have to do is eat a little cinnamon toast, and voila. Instant spermicide."

While Attain had wondered why cinnamon toast was always available at breakfast, he hadn't asked about it. He also hadn't touched it. "I'm allergic," he whispered when he finally had enough oxygen in his lungs to speak. His voice came out raspy, and he took another deep breath.

"Well, I hear the gargoyles can take it, too, and it has the same effect," Spieron told him. "Just tell Ssimeas to eat it."

Attain nodded. "Right. Okay."

Spieron slid his hand down Attain's spine, then back up it again. "Just continue to breathe. Everything will be okay."

Nodding again, Attain did just that. Slowly, the tightness in his chest eased, and he no longer felt like he was going to pass out. His body still trembled a little, and he would have been embarrassed for another man to see him like this, except —

I have a damn good reason for it.

"We could, we could have, have . . . *kids* together," Attain whispered, trying to wrap his brain around the information. "That's . . . biologically insane."

"I thought the same thing the first time I heard it, and I'm a vampire," Spieron confided. "I've not seen it happen myself, but I've heard of it, and it wouldn't be kids, technically."

Attain slid down the wall, allowing his trembling legs a break. "What would they be then?" Resting his head against the wall, he turned and peered at Spieron. "Half-breeds?"

Spieron settled next to him, his back against the wall. "No. Paranormal genes always win out over a human's." He rested his forearms on his upturned knees and offered him a commiserating smile. "All gargoyles are male. If a gargoyle has a male fated mate, all their offspring will be male, too." Then his brows furrowed, and his expression turned vacant. "And they will lay an egg."

Gaping once more, Attain let out a strangled sound. "L-Lay an e-egg?" Once again, black spots flashed across his vision, and he found himself having trouble catching his breath.

"Whoa, whoa," Spieron cried. The vampire again gripped the back of his neck and pushed his head down between his knees. "Gods, I just keep putting my foot in it."

"N-Needed to know," Attain mumbled. "Wh-Why wouldn't" — he panted a few more breaths — "they t-tell me?"

"Tell you what?" asked a deep voice. "And why are you sitting on the floor of that stall with your hands all over another man?"

Peering through his lashes, Attain spotted Albert. Spieron's huge partner had his eyes narrowed, and his forearms resting on the stall wall. Even through his neatly trimmed beard, the tension in his jaw was on clear display.

"Sorry, my beloved," Spieron crooned. "I dropped a bombshell on Attain and am doing my best to help him through it." His voice turned husky as he continued, "You know you're the only man for me."

"I know," Albert replied, his tone softening, as did his stance. He moved to the open door and strode into the stall. "What bombshell?" he asked as he knelt on the floor before Attain. Cradling his jaw in one big, work-roughened hand, Albert gave him a fatherly smile. "You know we're all here to help you through this."

Attain closed his eyes and sighed before whispering, "Thank you."

When was the last time my father looked at me that way or gave me such reassurance?

He couldn't remember.

For several seconds, Attain soaked up the comfort the pair offered him. Spieron continued to rub his back, stopping at his nape at each repetition to massage there before repeating. Albert slid his hand from Attain's jaw to scratch lightly at his scalp.

Finally, Attain reopened his eyes and met Albert's gaze. "Is it true that gargoyles can get their male mates pregnant?" It wasn't that he didn't trust Spieron. It was just he still struggled with the concept.

Albert glanced at Spieron before refocusing on him. "It is. But remember, Ssimeas is your mate and will always have your happiness at heart." Kneeling before Attain, he cupped his chin and leveled a serious look upon him. "Ssimeas would never force you to carry an egg. The choice to have a hatchling will always be left with you."

Swallowing hard, Attain straightened and returned his back to the wall, pulling from the other men. "Hatchlings." He focused on Spieron. "That's what you meant by it not really being a kid."

Spieron nodded. "Yes, although it's still your little one."

Still in shock, Attain couldn't help but ask, "A man carrying an egg. How does that even work?"

After flopping onto his butt, Albert rested his forearms on his knees. Then he explained.

CHAPTER EIGHT

Coming out of roost, Ssimeas inhaled deeply . . . and just held in a moan. The scent of his mate permeated the loft space. He lifted his head and spotted Attain sitting cross-legged on one of the pallets Nicholas had set up.

"Attain," Ssimeas whispered. When Attain just continued to stare at him with furrowed brows, Ssimeas slowly rose from his crouch. "Attain?" he asked worriedly as he slowly moved toward his mate. "I am happy to see you, but why are you here?"

"You can get me pregnant?"

Ssimeas froze upon hearing Attain's wary tone.

Oh, fuck me. Yep, that's one of the things I forgot to explain to my mate.

Licking his lips, Ssimeas continued forward. He settled on the pallet next to Attain as he thought about one explanation after another, discarding each one just as quickly. Instead, Ssimeas realized he needed to be open and honest.

"There is always so much to explain when introducing a human to the world of paranormals," Ssimeas began slowly. Taking a chance, he reached over and gripped Attain's hand. "So many things are different." To his pleasure, his mate didn't pull away, so he threaded their fingers together. "I didn't mean to leave anything out, and yes, male pregnancy is a big one. Please forgive me."

Attain stared at their joined hands for one heartbeat, then two, before he turned his head and peered at him. "You didn't answer my question."

Ssimeas nodded once, realizing his mate was right. "I'm sorry, Attain." He squeezed his mate's hand. "Yes, a gargoyle has the ability to impregnate his male fated mate, once they've completed their bond."

Nodding slowly, Attain returned his focus to the floor. "And to complete our bond" — while his words were slow and measured, they held a firm understanding — "we fuck and spill into each other and exchange blood."

"Yes," Ssimeas rumbled softly, squeezing Attain's hand once more. Then he tugged at him, earning his mate's focus. "But I much prefer using the term making love."

Attain's lips twitched, a hint of a smile appearing for an instant and disappearing just as quickly. "Your sperm could cause my appendix to turn into a womb, of sorts, and that's where your egg will form."

"*Our* egg," Ssimeas couldn't help but interject. Upon seeing Attain's lifted brows, he added, "Any child will be a mixture of both our DNAs. Our child. Our hatchling." Ssimeas realized what he'd said, so he had to explain. "Because gargoyles hatch from eggs, we call them hatchlings."

Humming softly, Attain nodded once more. "Then I lay it." He glanced Ssimeas's way before refocusing on the floor. "Out my ass."

Ssimeas cringed at the mental image those blunt words portrayed. "Yes." He wasn't going to lie to his mate.

Attain nodded slowly. "But it's easy to block, to uh . . . keep your semen from . . . you know." He waved his free hand in a vacant manner as his cheeks took on a pinkish hue. "You know what I mean."

Sighing, Ssimeas knew he had to come clean, and to do that, he had to shoot straight with his mate. "Someone told you by eating cinnamon, it would render my sperm infertile." Seeing Attain nod, Ssimeas remembered his mate's absent comment when he'd walked into the family room the week before. "And you're allergic?"

"Yeah. Sorry." Attain winced. "Never thought I'd be sorry about that before." He shrugged as he curved his lips into a wry smile. "Other than missing out on cinnamon rolls, never thought much about it."

"I'm sorry, my mate. There is a problem with that."

"What do you mean?" Attain cocked his head, then gaped. "Don't tell me you're allergic to cinnamon, too!"

Ssimeas quickly shook his head. "I'm not allergic . . . however—" He paused, then moved to kneel before Attain. "While it is not common, there are a few gargoyles whose seed is *not* sterilized by cinnamon." Wincing, Ssimeas brought Attain's hand to his lips. Before gently nipping his knuckle, he admitted, "I am one of those. Cinnamon does not work on me."

"I-It doesn't?" Attain reared back, his body flooding with tension. "B-But Sp-Spieron said—"

Lifting his free hand, Ssimeas gently put it over Attain's mouth, ceasing his stammering. "I'm sorry, my mate. So sorry. Normally, the vampire's information would have been true, but"—he paused and sighed—"I'm a rare case."

Attain nodded slowly, his eyebrows furrowing as he stared at the ground. "I get it," he whispered. Then he met Ssimeas's gaze. "Kinda like birth control commercials for women. It's not always perfect, so as they rattle off the fine print, something about safe sex practices and using condoms is always in there."

"Exactly." Ssimeas felt a measure of relief as he heard Attain's words.

Huffing a sigh, Attain cast a crooked smile his way. "So . . . we're gonna have to find another way, because no way am I anywhere near ready to be a baby oven," he stated, scrubbing his free hand over his scalp. "What did you all do before you discovered the cinnamon thing? Otherwise, we're gonna have to invest in a condom company, because I'm damn tired of my right hand, and it's only been a week."

"It's, ah, you, condom—" Realizing he was making no sense, he snapped his mouth shut. He even rocked back and sat on his ass. "You're accepting me? Why? What changed?"

Holy fucking shit! Did I just ask that?

Jerking his head to the side, Ssimeas growled low under his breath. "Gods, I can't believe I just said that, even if I am wondering."

To Ssimeas's relief, Attain chuckled . . . actually chuckled!

"It wasn't any one thing," Attain admitted, smiling at him. "You listened to Nicholas's guidance." He rolled his eyes. "Damn near embarrassed the shit out of me with that singing telegram yesterday, but the office workers got a kick out of it." His cheeks darkened to a reddish hue. "Father hated it, which means it was good." Then Attain nibbled his lower lip and met his gaze. His baby blues narrowed before he whispered, "He's going to make trouble."

Ssimeas nodded as he scrambled forward. Settling back beside Attain on the pallet, he once again took Attain's hand. "He can make trouble, but we'll deal with it." He winked. "We paranormals have plenty of special talents."

Attain scoffed. "So I've heard."

Shaking his head, Ssimeas told him. "I've heard over and over again this week that your father is pushing you to marry Chrissy." Upon seeing Attain's face color, he knew his hunch was right. He wrapped his wing around his mate and pulled him close as he dipped his head and whispered, "Do you have any idea how much anger I had to control whenever that was pointed out to me?"

To Ssimeas's pleasure, Attain rested his weight against him. He doubted his mate even realized that he snuggled against him. Ssimeas wasn't going to look a gift horse in the mouth.

"Paranormals are possessive," Attain mumbled absently.

"That we are," Ssimeas confirmed. "So." He pressed a kiss to Attain's jaw before whispering huskily into his ear, "How about after we bond, and I go through molt, you marry *me*?"

"Marry *you*?" Attain asked, clearly shocked as he whipped his head around to peer at him with his mouth agape. "Really?"

Ssimeas practically purred at the idea. "It is legal everywhere in this country now."

"M-Marry you," Attain repeated slowly. His grip tightened on Ssimeas's hand as his eyes turned a little vacant. "My father will fire me. I'll be disowned."

That wasn't a no.

Still, Attain sounded upset, uneasy, and Ssimeas wanted his mate happy and content. Easing his hand from Attain's, he wrapped his arm around his waist, instead. He also tucked his wings around his struggling human before dipping his head and nuzzling his temple.

Then Ssimeas began to trill. The deep vibrating originated in his chest and came out of his slightly parted lips, causing a low rumbling noise to fill the space. He continued to press light, open-mouthed kisses to Attain's jawline as he waited for the acrid, panicky scent to ease from his mate.

Attain sagged against him and let out a deep sigh. Turning his head, he met Ssimeas's lips. He took Ssimeas's mouth in a deep kiss, thrusting in his tongue and lapping along his sharp teeth.

Ssimeas released a low moan, ceasing his trilling, as he allowed Attain to explore him. Rubbing his hands down his mate's torso, he reached the hem of his t-shirt and slid his palms underneath. The feel of Attain's smooth skin beneath his fingers created a fire in his gut that threatened to swiftly burn away any semblance of his control.

He wanted that so badly.

Except —

Easing the kiss to an end, Ssimeas rasped, "Attain, my

mate, my soul" — scraping the tips of his claws along his human's spine, he watched a shiver work through him — "I wish to lay you down so badly." Seeing the slightly glazed gleam in Attain's eyes, Ssimeas pulled one hand free and threaded it through his mate's thick, light-brown hair. "But once we start, I don't know if I'll be able to stop until we have satisfied each and every one of our urges. We will enjoy each other's bodies, fuck each other and exchange blood, and be left sweaty and sated beyond anything we've ever before experienced."

Attain's lips curved into a hungry smile, his lips slightly swollen from Ssimeas's kisses. "If you're trying to deter me from thinking with my dick" — he glanced down pointedly at the large bulge behind his fly before returning his focus to him — "then you're not doing a very good job."

Ssimeas licked his lips, and his mouth watered. He wanted to see what Attain was packing in the worst way. Scraping his hand down his mate's neck, he began tracing his claws downward, so he could do just that.

Then Ssimeas groaned and jerked his focus back to Attain's smug expression. "If we do this, we will be bound for eternity," he warned bluntly. "We will be one. I will be yours, and you will be mine." Ssimeas narrowed his eyes as he warned, "And it can never be undone."

Attain licked his lips as he nodded slowly. "I understand that, Ssimeas." Lifting his hands, he placed them on Ssimeas's torso. "And I accept that." He paused a moment, nibbling his bottom lip and furrowing his brows. "I—"

When Attain didn't finish after a few heartbeats, Ssimeas cradled his mate's jaw as he teased over the skin of his ribcage. "Please, talk to me, Attain."

"You'll have to fuck me first. Then I'll fuck you because there's no way I'm gonna risk getting pregnant." Then Attain lifted his hand and waved his finger under Ssimeas's nose.

"Then if you ever want to fuck me after that, we use condoms."

Just hearing the words *fuck me* caused Ssimeas's stiff cock
to jerk within the confines of his loincloth. His stomach
clenched with need, and he gritted his teeth to fight back a
groan. Then he actually processed Attain's words, and his
breath caught in his chest.

My mate is offering me everything.

Well, almost.

"There are old ways to render me infertile," Ssimeas stated.
"They just haven't been used in centuries. I will look into it."
Seeing the narrowing of Attain's eyes, he quickly added, "Un-
til then, after we bond, we will use condoms."

Attain dipped his chin in a swift nod. "Okay, then." He
grabbed the hem of his t-shirt and whipped it over his head.
Once his face reappeared and, as he tossed the fabric off the
side of the pallet, Attain grinned cockily at him. "Let's get this
party started."

On board with that, Ssimeas growled low in his throat. He
grabbed Attain's hips and shoved him back a bit, then pushed
him so he reclined on the pallet. "Lie down, my mate," he ordered roughly. As soon as Attain obeyed, resting his weight
on his elbows, Ssimeas trailed his fingertips down the defined
line that ran between his mate's pectorals. "So handsome," he
rumbled, exploring his abdominals. When Ssimeas reached
the button-fly of Attain's jeans, he lifted his gaze to meet his
human's. Seeing his new and forever lover's flushed face and
heavy-lidded eyes, he grinned. "You are gorgeous in your
need, my mate."

Attain gave him a sultry grin. "Better do something quick,"
he ordered, reaching into his pocket and pulling out a small
tube of lubricant. "Or I'm gonna finish without you." As Attain held it out, he began skimming the fingertips of his free
hand across his chest so he could tweak his own nipple. "I
haven't gone this long without sex in a long time, Ssimeas, so

you better damn well deliver."

Upon hearing Attain speak of past exploits, even obliquely, Ssimeas snarled. His possessiveness roared through him. Narrowing his eyes, he grabbed the lube from his mate as he untied his loincloth with the other. Whipping the fabric from his hips, Ssimeas revealed his heavy, thick shaft.

"Never speak of your past lovers to me again, Attain," Ssimeas warned. Using his thumb to pop the cap on the lube, he palmed himself and gave his erection a light stroke. "You are mine, and I will please you. Make no mistake of that."

Upon seeing Attain's eyes dilate and his jaw sagging open, even his breathing switched to panting breaths, Ssimeas felt a surge of satisfaction filling him. His mate needed him just as much as he craved his human. While they'd only met a week before, the need to complete their bond worked fast.

Yep. Don't mess with Fate's plans.

"Take those pants off, Attain," Ssimeas ordered, desiring to see his mate naked before him. "Or you may not have them for later." His fingers twitched with his wish to shred the offending articles of clothing, removing them from his human's body. "Let me see you."

Grinning widely, Attain kicked off his boots. "You gonna ravish me, my gargoyle?" He bent at the waist and yanked off his socks. After tossing them toward his boots, Attain reached for his fly. "Gonna eat me up?"

"Oh, I will definitely eat you," Ssimeas rumbled as images of licking and sucking Attain's cock, balls, and ass flooded his mind. "Can't wait to make you scream with need and beg for my cock."

Ssimeas remembered Attain's admittance of loving ass play. As he watched his human kick off his jeans and underwear, revealing his strong, leanly muscled body to his hungry gaze, Ssimeas thought of all the ways he could capitalize on that. He licked his lips upon seeing Attain's swollen shaft stretch from his groin to hover over his stomach. The pearl of pre-cum he saw ooze up from it made his mouth water for a taste.

"Shit, never had anyone look at me like that," Attain whispered, drawing Ssimeas's attention back to his face. "Y-You really wanna suck me, don't you?"

Chuckling huskily, Ssimeas winked at Attain as he crawled onto the pallet. "Oh, yes, my mate." He pushed Attain's legs, spreading them wide. Attain's stomach clenched, but he didn't resist, sending Ssimeas's anticipation soaring. "And gonna do plenty more than that."

Then Ssimeas skimmed the claws of his forefingers up Attain's straining erection just to see it bob beneath his touch.

The moan Attain let out caused Ssimeas's heart to thud wildly in his chest. When the bead of pre-cum began to slide along Attain's crown, he couldn't resist. Ssimeas opened his mouth, gripped the base of his human's erection to steady it, and lapped across his flesh.

Attain's light flavor burst across Ssimeas's taste buds, and he groaned. Needing more, he wrapped his lips around his mate's shaft and swallowed him to the root.

CHAPTER NINE

Attain sucked in a harsh gasp as he felt his throbbing cock being encased in the most exquisite sucking sensation he'd ever experienced. Propped on his elbows, staring at Ssimeas, he met the gargoyle's gaze. His dark-gray eyes gleamed with something Attain couldn't identify as he peered right back at him.

Then Ssimeas's lips curved into an obscene smile where they were wrapped around Attain's erection. He began to suck up, easing partway off his dick, then sank down again. When he did it once more, Ssimeas teased at Attain's frenulum, and Attain couldn't contain his groan.

Tipping his head back, Attain allowed it to hang, trapping his bottom lip with his teeth to stifle his cries of delight, as he experienced the most exquisite fellatio of his life. The gargoyle licked over his crown, teased at the wrinkled skin beneath it, and even dipped his tongue into his slit. He did all that between strong sucking bobs that stimulated the sensitive skin of his erection.

His gut clenched, his blood fired in his veins, and his nipples ached for touch, but Attain didn't move for fear Ssimeas would stop the exquisite torture.

Just as Attain felt his swollen balls begin to tighten and the tingle began at the base of his spine, the sensations all stopped as Ssimeas released him.

Attain let out a whine of dismay that he would forever deny. Snapping his head back up, he opened eyes he didn't remember closing and gazed at Ssimeas. The gargoyle winked, then stuck out his tongue and lapped at his balls.

Squeaking in surprise, Attain shuddered. Then his arms gave out, and he flopped onto his back. Feeling another long swipe from the base of his balls and all around his sack, Attain couldn't hold back his moan of pleasure.

"There's the noises I want to hear," Ssimeas crooned before gently suckling one orb into his mouth.

"Oh god!" Attain cried, gaping at the gargoyle. "You're sucking my nuts."

"Mmm-hmm," Ssimeas hummed, the vibration transferring to Attain's testicles.

"Ssim!" Attain tried to stay still, but his hips jolted and his thighs trembled, beyond his control. "Oh fuck!"

Ssimeas clamped one black-clawed hand on his hip as he drew off his balls.

Attain whined in dismay. "Please," he whimpered, meeting the male's smug gaze. "So close."

"Then come," Ssimeas urged as he gripped Attain's thigh with his other hand. Then he dipped his head again.

Instead of sucking his balls, however, Ssimeas used his hold on Attain's leg and hip to lift and spread him further. He almost protested, feeling exposed in a way he'd never felt before. Except, then Ssimeas stuck out his tongue and swiped down his cleft.

Attain barked a harsh cry as he felt Ssimeas's mobile appendage slide across the sensitive skin of his pucker. Feeling the gargoyle nuzzle his nose into the back of his balls while continuing to work the skin of his star, he moaned and gripped the sheet beneath him. His body ignited as new and delicious sensations shot through him.

When Ssimeas pushed his tongue into Attain's channel, he lost it. His balls pulled tight so fast it took his breath away. His throbbing erection pulsed, spurting stream after stream, but Ssimeas didn't stop. He continued to lick, suck, and nibble at Attain's entrance while thrusting his tongue deep inside his body.

Attain cried Ssimeas's name as his orgasm continued on and on. Shivering and trembling in the gargoyle's hold, he saw spots dance across his vision. He struggled to get enough air into his lungs.

Only when Attain whimpered, "Ssimeas, please," did the gargoyle lift his head.

"Oh, my mate," Ssimeas crooned as he lowered Attain's ass back to the sheet. "You look gorgeous in your pleasure."

Then Attain felt it. He didn't know when it had happened, but there was still something in his chute. When Ssimeas pulled it out and pushed it back into him, Attain realized it was the gargoyle's thick finger.

Attain instinctively clenched around it, but it didn't hurt. "Nice." Having fingered his own ass enough times, he sighed and rocked into the sensation. "Different than my own," he muttered, slurring slightly.

Ssimeas smiled down at him as he grabbed the tube of lube where he'd dropped it on the sheet at some point. "It will only get better," he assured as he poured some onto his fingers and Attain's hole.

Flinching at the slight chill, Attain winced.

"Sorry, Attain," Ssimeas murmured, swiping his tongue across his abdominals, the warmth of his tongue leaving a trail of tingles behind. "It'll warm soon."

"Mmm-hmm," Attain muttered. He'd used lube plenty of times. "It's the warming kind."

Ssimeas hummed as he licked along the groove of one of his abdominals. "Nice," he mumbled, continuing to clean Attain's release from him with his tongue. "Taste so good." As soon as Attain met Ssimeas's gaze, the gargoyle asked, "Why did you change your mind, my mate?"

Attain felt Ssimeas slide his claw ever-so-lightly against his prostate. A flash of pleasure-pain spiked through his groin, nearly causing his eyes to roll to the back of his head. Gritting his teeth, he rocked into the touch as Ssimeas pulled his finger out a little, then pushed it back in again.

"Hmmm?" Ssimeas pressed softly as he eased a second finger in beside the first. "Why, my handsome human?"

"Fucking hell," Attain grunted out, as he scowled at Ssimeas. "You w-want to t-talk about this n-now?"

Ssimeas paused where he licked his way up Attain's chest. Sweeping his gaze over Attain's face, he grinned. Something in Attain's expression must have given him some kind of answer.

"You're right, Attain," Ssimeas stated around a wide, feral smile. "But I will ask you again later." Then he rubbed over Attain's prostate again. "For now . . . just feel."

As if Attain could do anything else, for right then, Ssimeas began assaulting his prostate with each push and pull. He coupled that with licks, nips, and sucks to his torso. When Ssimeas reached his beaded nipples, Attain moaned wantonly.

Attain shuddered and shivered under the gargoyle's ministrations. He arched and twitched. Planting his feet, he pushed into each move his new lover made.

Never in his wildest imaginings would he have thought sex could feel like this. He'd always been the strong one in the pairing, the one who made certain his touch gave pleasure. Never had he been able to just lie back and enjoy.

He knew he could so easily get addicted to Ssimeas's touch.

Even as the thought tripped through his mind, Attain realized there was nothing wrong with that. The huge beast was his mate, his forever partner. The idea caused his heart rate to spike for a whole new reason.

"Easy, Attain," Ssimeas purred, rubbing his free hand along his thigh. He teased around his balls as he met Attain's gaze. "Whatever it is, we can talk it through. What just caused you to tense up?"

Licking his lips, Attain met Ssimeas's gaze. "I—" He bit back his automatic response of, *I'm fine*. Attain knew he needed to be honest. "I want a relationship with you, Ssimeas." Attain's voice came out a rough whisper, but he forged ahead. "I might freak out a little about it from time to time. My trust button is sorta broken."

Ssimeas smiled at him. "Thank you for sharing with me, Attain." He nuzzled over Attain's nipple, drawing a moan from Attain's throat. "I can't promise that I won't make mistakes. I've never been in a relationship, either." Easing upward, Ssimeas nibbled at the tendon running up the side of Attain's neck. "But I've been waiting for you for a long time, Attain, so I will do my best to fix whatever problems arise between us." Then he lifted his head and peered at him with a serious expression. "All I ask is that you do the same. Can you do that, Attain?"

Attain nodded. "Yes, Ssimeas." Releasing the sheet, he reached for the gargoyle, wrapping his arms around his wide shoulders. "I made that decision before coming here."

Ssimeas's smile was wide and full of teeth. Attain figured he should have been afraid of all those pointy pearly-whites, seeing as the gargoyle had told him he would bite him. For some reason, however, Attain found himself turned on.

He'd always enjoyed a little pain with his pleasure.

"Hurry, Ssimeas," Attain urged, sliding his hands up to the back of the gargoyle's neck. "I'm ready."

"You're really not," Ssimeas countered, a smirk toying at the corners of his lips. "I'm a big gargoyle, Attain." He waggled his eyebrow ridges as he lowered his head. Then Ssimeas whispered into Attain's ear, "Everywhere."

Attain couldn't help but peer down between their bodies. Upon seeing the massive rod jutting from Ssimeas's groin, he sucked in a harsh gasp. The male had to be at least ten inches of dark-blue, thick flesh. His foreskin was nearly fully retracted, revealing a shiny bulbous crown that leaked pre-cum onto the sheet beneath them.

"O-Okay." Attain gulped as he watched the massive piece of meat twitch. "Maybe I do need a third finger."

Ssimeas's chuckle sounded rough. "Good idea. Now let me finish prepping you."

Attain would have griped at the gargoyle for laughing at him, but then the male latched onto the sensitive bit of skin behind his ear. Instead, he moaned, turned his head, and welcomed the sensations cascading through him. The hairs on his nape stood on end, and goose bumps erupted on his skin.

"So good," Attain mumbled as Ssimeas's fingers once again rubbed over his prostate. His brain began to shut down. "Oh, god, more!"

Ssimeas didn't disappoint. The gargoyle played his body like he was born to do it. Hell, with all their talk of mates and joining of souls, maybe he had been.

Then Attain's brain shut down. All he could do was feel. His body felt on fire, and his cock once again throbbed. His balls rolled pleasantly, his nipples ached deliciously, and his gut clenched as he struggled to control the sudden need to orgasm again.

Just when Attain didn't think he would be able to control himself a second longer, Ssimeas released the nipple he'd been working and eased his fingers from Attain's chute.

Attain whimpered, "No!"

"Not until I'm in you, my mate," Ssimeas rasped. He gripped Attain's hips and squeezed. When Attain blinked open bleary eyes and peered up at him, Ssimeas told him, "First times are easier on your hands and knees. Would you like to roll over?"

Would I?

Even though Attain really wanted to peer into Ssimeas's

eyes as they coupled, he remembered the log that jutted from the gargoyle's groin.

"I'll roll over."

Ssimeas rocked backward, then helped Attain to roll over.

As Attain drew his knees under, he felt Ssimeas skim his palms down his back. When the gargoyle's hands reached his ass, a tremble worked down his spine. Feeling Ssimeas grip his mounds, a wave of anticipation rolled through Attain even as his gut clenched.

"Relax," Ssimeas urged as he pried Attain's cheeks apart. "Remember to push out."

Attain felt something blunt and thick press against his opening, and he instinctively clenched.

Ssimeas levered over him, bracketing his body. Between the kisses he rained up his neck, he crooned, "I have you, my mate. Only wish to give you pleasure." Reaching under him, Ssimeas gripped his erection, which had flagged a smidge due to his sudden rise in nerves. "Push out, and let me in."

Feeling Ssimeas's calloused fingers sliding along his length, Attain sighed. He lowered to his elbows and canted his hips. While he fisted his hands, he concentrated on pushing out and relaxing his clenching chute muscles.

"That's the way," Ssimeas encouraged, stroking him. His erection also pressed harder against his star. "Remember to keep breathing."

Attain snapped, "I'll breathe when you hurry the fuck up." Peering over his shoulder, he scowled at the huge male preparing to mount him. "I'm not made of glass."

"I still want you to enjoy this," Ssimeas responded huskily, his gray eyes the color of storm clouds. "I want you to crave me just as much as I crave you."

Before Attain could come up with a response, Ssimeas lurched forward and sealed his lips over Attain's in an awkward kiss. He opened to the gargoyle's questing tongue. It wasn't until after Ssimeas had sunk his mobile appendage deep into his mouth and he tasted the slight musk coating the gargoyle's normally masculine flavor that he remembered where that appendage had been.

Instead of pulling away, Attain gave a mental shrug and kissed Ssimeas back.

Then Ssimeas thrust his hips, and Attain felt his guardian muscle give way. Grunting, he couldn't stop his body from tensing. Ssimeas broke the kiss and nuzzled his lips down his neck.

"Push out," Ssimeas reminded as he continued jacking his dick in long, languorous strokes. "Long, slow breaths."

Doing as Ssimeas instructed, Attain inhaled and exhaled, focusing on relaxing his channel. He rested his forehead on one fist and pushed back against the gargoyle. He just knew if he could get Ssimeas's crown to slide over his prostate, all the pain from the stretch would disappear.

"That's the way, Attain," Ssimeas rumbled, his voice sounding strained. "Beg for my cock with your body. Gods, so good." Easing deeper, he muttered, "Your body was made to caress my length."

Attain finally felt it. Ssimeas's flared head slid over his prostate, causing the nerves of his channel to flare with fiery tingles. Moaning Ssimeas's name, Attain felt his erection once again throb.

"Attain," Ssimeas ground out. "Oh, Attain. Fuck!"

"Yeah," Attain replied, his own voice just as rough. "Yeah, that's what we want. To fuck." He sighed deeply when he felt Ssimeas's balls press against his own. His inner muscles were stretched impossibly wide, but for some reason, he no longer felt pain. Instead, it felt as if his nerve endings were lit up from the inside out. "Never knew what I was missin'. Damn!" Wriggling his ass a little, Attain felt Ssimeas's dick move a little within him, but he needed more. "Fuck me. Please fuck me."

"Anything my mate wants," Ssimeas replied before he began to move. "Gonna make you come from my touch, then from my bite."

Attain didn't think that was possible, but then Ssimeas began to nail his prostate over and over. Coupled with his hand massaging his dick as well as the way he sucked on his neck, Attain felt his balls begin to pull tight. He suddenly realized his overly stimulated body was going to come embarrassingly fast . . . and there wasn't a damn thing he could do about it.

Hell, he didn't even want to.

"Do it, my mate," Ssimeas crooned into his ear before scraping a sharp tooth over the sensitive skin behind it. "I can feel you trembling. Give in."

Then Ssimeas adjusted his angle and slowed his ruts. His cock head rested on Attain's prostate, creating unending waves of pleasure-pain to roll through him.

Attain roared with bliss as his balls unloaded. His gut clenched as his chute muscles contracted and relaxed around the massive rod invading him. He shivered with the intensity of his release, and sweat beaded on his skin.

Ssimeas pushed as deep as possible once again, clutching Attain close, as he wrapped his mouth around the point where his neck met his shoulder.

When Ssimeas bit, pain lanced through him, and Attain opened his mouth to cry out in surprise. Then the sensation morphed into the most erotic of tingles, and Attain found himself blindsided by a third orgasm in so short a time.

His senses overloaded, and he couldn't help it when his eyes rolled back and darkness took him.

CHAPTER TEN

Ssimeas felt Attain's body go limp beneath him. Releasing his lover's softening prick, he banded his arm around his chest, holding him in place. After enjoying another gulp of Attain's blood, rolling the iron-rich flavor across the hundreds of receptors on his tongue, he hummed contentedly.

Then Ssimeas eased his teeth from Attain's flesh. He swiped his tongue over his impressive bite mark, cleaning away the last bit of blood oozing from between the punctures. The move also sealed it, leaving behind a gorgeous claiming scar.

All mine.

Now I just need to rouse my mate and get him to claim me.

Ssimeas knew a fun way to do it, too.

Ever-so-carefully, Ssimeas eased his still-hard dick from Attain's chute. He couldn't wait to experience his mate's body again, but he had promises to keep first. To that end, Ssimeas lowered Attain to the pallet, being careful to position him out of the wet spot.

Rolling Attain onto his back, Ssimeas grinned at the languid smile curving his sleeping human's lips. He gently spread his lover's legs as he grabbed the lube. After pouring a dollop of the slick onto the tip of his tail, he set it aside.

Then Ssimeas knelt over Attain's groin and began cleaning him . . . with his tongue. At the same time, he eased his tail into his own channel. He sighed softly as he stretched himself, all the while wallowing in Attain's musky scent and the taste of his own semen.

Even the flavor of the lube mingled in didn't detract in the least.

As Ssimeas worked, he felt Attain's prick thicken under his tongue's ministrations. His own cock bobbed between his legs, even though he did his best to avoid his prostate. He wanted to be stretched and aroused, not on the edge.

Attain's soft moan and the shifting of his legs told Ssimeas his mate was rousing.

Ssimeas tipped his gaze upward, admiring his human's strong lines. His delineated six-pack led to the defined lines of his pectorals. Even his arms displayed wonderful biceps and triceps.

I want to lick every inch of him.

Eyelashes fluttering, Attain peeled open his eyes and peered down his body at him. His lips curved into a satiated smile. Then Ssimeas swiped his tongue up Attain's length, and joy flooded him upon hearing his human's low moan and upon seeing the twist of pleasure-pain on his face.

"Oh, god," Attain mumbled, discomfort clear in his tone. "How can I be hard again?"

Finally lifting his head, Ssimeas peered down at his lover. "Because we're not done, yet, Attain." Upon scenting his mate's confusion, he reminded him, "You still need to claim me, remember?"

Attain sucked in a harsh gasp as his jaw sagged open. Then his eyes took on a hungry gleam. He licked his lips as he swept his gaze over Ssimeas.

"Hell yeah," Attain whispered, reaching down to palm his dick. "God I want to rub one out all over your wings."

Ssimeas felt his dick twitch at that visual. Shivering, he nodded slowly. For some reason, that idea didn't turn him off, not at all.

"I can't think of anything that would please me more than you marking me with your seed," Ssimeas admitted, a shudder working through him. His breathing hitched, and his blood burned in his veins. "The idea of carrying your scent on my skin, so others will be able to smell you upon me . . . oh gods." Ssimeas groaned as he reached down and gripped the base of his aching shaft. "So fucking sexy."

But first —

Snapping open eyelids Ssimeas hadn't realized he'd closed, he groaned. "I need you to claim me first."

"Y-Yeah."

With impressive coordination, since just a few seconds before Attain had seemed out of it, his mate rolled to his knees and grabbed the discarded bottle of lube. "God, I've never gone without a condom before." He squirted some onto his palm, then gripped his length and coated his erection. "Can't wait to feel your tight heat squeeze me."

Ssimeas found himself mesmerized by the way Attain jacked himself. The human's crown appeared red and swollen, and each time he slid his fingers to the base, his slit gaped. His arm muscles seemed to quiver as if he were barely keeping himself in check.

"Turn around, Ssimeas," Attain ordered, yanking his attention back to his lover's face, finding it flushed and heavy-lidded. "I gotta prepare you."

"Already done, my mate," Ssimeas admitted, easing his tail out from behind himself. He waggled the gleaming appendage in the air as he winked at his lover. "How do you want me?"

Attain opened his mouth, then closed it again.

Ssimeas thought he knew what his mate would want and was about to turn around, but his human surprised him.

"Lie on your back and spread your legs."

Doing as he'd been told, Ssimeas relaxed back onto the pallet's sheet. He spread his legs and stared up at Attain. Upon seeing the way his mate swept an appreciative gaze over him, a surge of pride filled Ssimeas.

"Your wings are so damn sexy, Ssimeas," Attain murmured as he eased between his legs. He met his gaze, asking, "Can I touch them?"

Grinning, extremely pleased that Attain found his differences enticing, Ssimeas nodded. "You may touch me anywhere, my mate." He lifted his hand, palm up, as he told him, "I am yours."

Attain reached out and took his hand, so Ssimeas tugged lightly, so he fell forward. His mate's free hand landed on the bed. Ssimeas guided the hand he held to his wing, where he'd draped some of it over the tops of his shoulders. The rest he'd tucked under him, since he'd been worried Attain would be intimidated by them.

So glad he's not.

When Attain began petting down the leathery appendage, Ssimeas bit back a groan. His mate's fingertips stroking over his sensitive flesh felt absolutely exquisite. It caused tingles to spread through his chest, and his nipples beaded.

"Wow," Attain murmured. "So much softer than I thought it'd be."

Then, realizing he shouldn't be hiding anything from his mate, he let out a long low moan. His wings fluttered where they half-covered his chest, damn near out of his control. His cock twitched, and pre-cum oozed from him.

"Oh, damn." Attain hummed appreciatively before his voice lowered to a husky tenor. "Your wings are sensitive."

"Oh, yes," Ssimeas managed to find his tongue. "N-Never touch another's wings. It's considered rude to touch without permission," he warned. Then he added, "The tail, too."

Attain stopped rubbing his wing in favor of sitting up to peer at Ssimeas's tail where he had it wrapped around his left thigh. "Really?"

Ssimeas held his breath even as he nodded.

Placing the forefingers of his right hand on Ssimeas's tail, Attain slowly stroked down it.

"A-Attain!" Ssimeas moaned, and his tail twitched, threatening to uncoil. When Attain teased over the short bit he could reach once again, Ssimeas hissed, and his erection pulsed. "Please, Attain," he begged. "I need you."

"God, that is so fucking sexy," Attain muttered. "It's really arousing for you, isn't it?"

Ssimeas nodded. "Oh, yeah."

As Attain levered over him, gripping his dick and guiding it to his hole, he grinned widely at Ssimeas. "So, tell me" — he bumped his cock's crown to Ssimeas's lubed hole — "do you think I could get you off by playing with your wings and tail?"

Groaning just at the thought, Ssimeas nodded. "Probably."

"God, that would be sexy." Attain gave him a feral grin. "You could lie on your stomach as I jack off on your back. Then I'll massage my cum into your wings and over your tail." When Ssimeas groaned at the imagery, Attain's expression turned predatory. "You like that idea, don't you?"

"I do," Ssimeas admitted, his breath coming in harsh pants. "So fucking much."

"Another time," Attain promised.

Ssimeas nodded eagerly. He could hardly wait. Lifting his arms, he beckoned with his fingers.

"Take me," Ssimeas encouraged, wriggling his hips, hoping to stimulate Attain's crown and encourage him to thrust. When his mate still hesitated, Ssimeas purred, "I need you, my mate."

Groaning, Attain levered over him and thrust.

Pushing out, Ssimeas willed his body to relax and accept his human into him. He felt his guardian muscle relax and stretch. In the next instant, he moaned in bliss.

My mate is inside me.

"A-Are you o-okay?" Attain rasped.

Ssimeas rested his hands on Attain's sides, then skimmed up his back, relishing the feel of his smooth flesh. "Oh, yes," he assured, smiling at his mate. "I am damn near perfect." Ssimeas gripped Attain's hips with his thighs. "Please fuck me, Attain. Spill in me." He figured he was begging, but he couldn't give a shit. "Drink my blood and complete our bond."

To Ssimeas's surprise, Attain sprawled over him. He reached up and gripped Ssimeas's horns, holding his head in place so their gazes locked. Then Attain gave him a devilish smile.

"Oh, I am going to do all those things and more, my gargoyle."

Ssimeas's breath caught in his chest when he heard his mate's possessiveness. *Gods, I love the sound of that.* The way Attain used his horns as leverage to rock his hips forward and sink deep inside Ssimeas's body was also sexy as fuck.

"Oh, yeah," Attain muttered under his breath. His sweat-slicked body moved above Ssimeas's own. "You feel so fantastic, Ssim."

Letting out a groan of his own, Ssimeas rocked his hips into each of Attain's thrusts. When his human adjusted his angle and pegged his prostate, he hissed and shuddered. Sparks shot through his rectum, sending starbursts of bliss through his groin.

Attain's grin appeared smug. "Found it."

"Hell yeah, you did." Ssimeas couldn't do anything about the whine in his voice. "Attain!"

His mate picked up his pace.

Trapped between the hold Attain had on his horns and the way he hammered his prostate, Ssimeas held on for the ride. He cupped his mate's shoulder blades and rocked into each move. His own dick rubbed between their bodies, leaking pre-cum like a sieve.

Never had Ssimeas allowed such mastery over him, but with it being his mate, he welcomed it. He reveled in it. His body damn near exploded with tingles as he felt Attain moving within him.

Ssimeas watched the feral grimace overtake Attain's face, and he groaned. The pleasure he saw written all over his mate skyrocketed his own enjoyment. Heat fired in his belly, and his balls began to draw up.

"Yeah, do it," Attain ordered as he began snapping his hips in earnest. "I wanna feel you clench on my cock. Do it now!"

Unable to deny his mate any more than he could resist the urge to breathe, Ssimeas felt his testicles tighten. His abdominals clenched as his cock throbbed. With a roar of delight, he soared on the endorphins pinging through his system.

The feel of Attain's release deep inside his body registered, refocusing Ssimeas's attention. Reaching between them, he scraped his claw across his chest, just above his heart. His blood welled up from the wound.

"Drink," Ssimeas urged. "Please, drink."

Without hesitation, Attain obeyed.

Feeling his mate latch onto his chest, Ssimeas moaned. He shivered at the sensation of Attain drinking from him. His cock spurted once again, and as he cradled his mate to his chest, another orgasm pulsed through him.

Ssimeas moaned Attain's name, and his lips curved into a sated smile. A moment later, he felt his mate's tongue slide across his pectoral. He figured his wound had closed, since a gargoyle's healing was so swift.

Peeling his eyelids open, Ssimeas stared at his mate. He saw Attain's cheek resting on his chest, but the human made no move to shift off him or pull away. Ssimeas liked that.

As Ssimeas rubbed up and down Attain's back, he sighed deeply. "Thank you, Attain," he whispered. "You have made me the happiest damn gargoyle on the planet."

Attain's chuckle sounded husky as he tipped his chin up

and met his gaze. His blue eyes were heavy-lidded, and his face was flushed. Ssimeas slid his claws through Attain's hair and pushed the sweat-dampened locks from his forehead.

"Think that's funny?" Ssimeas asked curiously, wondering what could possibly be running through his mate's mind.

"Not really, no," Attain admitted, his deep tenor soft and lethargic. He sighed deeply. "I just think I should be saying that to you, since I think I'm going to be bringing even more trouble to you, Nicholas, and your elder."

"Oh?" Ssimeas didn't like the smell of sadness coloring Attain's scent, especially after they'd just finished bonding. "How so?"

Attain's brows furrowed, and he swallowed hard enough to cause his Adam's apple to bob. "You're not gonna like this, but I have to be honest with you."

Ssimeas nodded. "Honesty is always best."

"Eh." Attain rolled his head in a bit of a waggle, but he didn't truly counter him. "I agreed to bond with you for several reasons. You're hot and turn me on like no one I've ever met. You're honest and straightforward." Holding his gaze with his own serious one, Attain added, "Plus, you won't ever cheat."

Holding his gaze, Ssimeas saw a myriad of emotions flash across his mate's blue eyes. "Trust is a tricky thing with you." He'd already known it but figured it couldn't hurt to reiterate it, proving he understood.

Attain nodded once as he whispered, "On top of that, my father set up another dinner date for me with Chrissy at his house tomorrow tonight. I told him no, but he set it up anyway." Attain's smile appeared pinched as he stated, "He's going to be pissed when I skip it."

"Then don't skip it," Ssimeas stated on a growl, his possessiveness flooding him. Upon seeing the way Attain's brows shot up, he added, "I will have gone through molt by then, so take me as your date instead."

Gaping, Attain stared up at him. "Seriously?" When Ssimeas just lifted one brow ridge, Attain smirked. "You'll be walking into the line of fire."

Ssimeas scoffed. "I've faced off against plenty worse than a stick-up-his-ass, bigoted asshole."

To Ssimeas's relief, Attain barked a laugh.

CHAPTER ELEVEN

Watching Ssimeas go through molt had been scary, but Attain felt even more fear now. He and his father hadn't ever had a real close relationship . . . not since his mother had died. Still, they'd always gotten along.

Not this time.

With the fingers of his left hand twined with Ssimeas's right and those of his other hand wrapped around the satchel he had slung over his right shoulder, Attain made his way toward the front door of his childhood home. As he moved, he couldn't help glancing at his human-looking lover. The gargoyle had changed so much, yet he still found him just as handsome and provocative.

Ssimeas still towered over him by several inches, leaving him standing about six-foot-six. His skin had lightened only a little, giving him African-style features. He still had broad shoulders, and his muscles bulged. The big difference—besides the lack of wings, pointy teeth, and claws—was that he had hair. For some reason, Ssimeas's huge black horns had spread and softened, creating wavy, shoulder-blade-length black hair.

Currently, the gargoyle had it pulled back into a queue at his nape, and Attain constantly fought with his desire to loosen it. Over the course of the day, he'd found he enjoyed running his fingers through it just as much as he loved petting Ssimeas's wings, tail, and horns. Attain had assured his surprisingly reticent gargoyle that he was attracted to him in either form.

That was when Attain had learned that most paranormals, gargoyles especially, didn't view attraction the same as humans did. Due to their heightened senses, paranormals were attracted primarily by scent as opposed to looks. Gargoyles, due to their different form, had a hard time understanding what humans found aesthetically pleasing.

Nicholas had urged Attain to compliment various features of both forms to reassure his lover. Appreciating the advice, Attain had done so, allowing him to soothe his new partner.

Partner. Damn. I have a partner, a mate.

The idea both thrilled Attain and scared the shit out of him. He still feared screwing up. After spending most of the day lying around the loft, chatting, exploring, and fucking with Ssimeas, however, Attain felt more secure.

"Relax, Attain," Nicholas assured from where he walked to his right. He and Bodb, as well as Sandra and Maggie, had joined them. "Things will work out." His buddy bumped his shoulder with his own. "At least opening an office of your own will lower your stress level."

As Attain inserted his key into the front door's lock, he arched one brow. "How do you figure? Now I'll have the added weight of handling all the paperwork myself as well as the eventual employee shit, getting new clients, and figuring out if my business is making ends meet for not just me, but employees . . . if I do get any." Upon realizing that he was rambling, he snapped his mouth shut. Just the thought caused a spike of anxiety to surge through him. "Shit."

"You don't have to worry about any of that," Ssimeas countered, his deep voice soothing as he squeezed Attain's fingers. "Hell, you don't have to do any cases you don't want to." Then he winked. "You landed yourself a very rich husband, my mate."

Gaping, Attain found himself standing stock-still in the middle of the home's large foyer. "Really?" He peered up into his big lover—that was another thing he was still getting used to, looking up at a lover—and cocked his head. Lowering his voice, Attain whispered, "How is that possible? What with the whole stone thing and all?"

Ssimeas must have realized what Attain was actually asking—*How could he have acquired a lot of wealth while living as a stone statue half his life?*

Chuckling, Ssimeas dipped his head and rumbled into his ear, "I may have lived half the day as a stone statue, but I have also been living a long, long time, Attain." Straightening a little so their gazes met, Ssimeas cradled Attain's jaw with his free hand. "It's a long time to accumulate wealth, and back when I started, it was in the form of shiny things and precious metals. Hell, if you don't want to work, at all, you never have to again."

Attain's brows shot up. "You essentially have a hoard? Like a dragon?"

Ssimeas barked a laugh. "Sure, handsome. Just like that."

"Damn." Wonder filled Attain. "How about that."

"Attain, is that you?"

His father's voice announced his approach just as surely as his heavy footsteps did.

"What's going on here? Who are all these people?" George demanded. His eyes were narrowed, and his gaze was riveted on where Attain and Ssimeas touched. "Who are you? Step away from my son and get out of my house."

When Attain turned to face his father fully, he decided to take the offensive. "Father, I'd like to go into your office and discuss an important matter that has come up." He waved toward the left stairwell and hall above it, hoping his father would lead the way.

Attain wasn't that lucky.

"Whatever it is can wait until after our dinner with your girlfriend and her father," George stated on a growl. Anger burned in his eyes as he again pinned his focus on Ssimeas. "Now, who is this man, and why are you holding his hand?"

Then George waved his hand as if brushing away his own questions. "Never mind. Release him, and leave," he demanded again.

"No, Father," Attain countered, shaking his head. He instinctively tightened his grip on Ssimeas. "I don't know how many times I have to tell you that I'm not dating Chrissy." Then he took the plunge and added, "This is Ssimeas. He's the one who's been sending gifts." Spinning the skewed version of events that they'd come up with to explain their sudden relationship, Attain told him, "We met at Nicholas's ranch and hit it off. When you started pressuring me to date Chrissy, Ssimeas began sending gifts to the office so you'd come to understand that I'm already seeing someone." Attain shook his head as he frowned at his glaring father. "I didn't realize you were a bigot, though, and would have such trouble accepting our relationship."

Curving his lips into a sneer, George stated, "No. This is in no way acceptable. You will cease this deviant behavior and take your place at Chrissy's side."

George crossed his arms over his chest, lifted his chin, and narrowed his eyes in a domineering expression that used to cause Attain's mouth to go dry and unease to slither through his gut. To his surprise, now it did nothing. Well, not nothing, actually. Instead, Attain realized all it did was accentuate how cold his father's eyes had become over the years as well as the growth of his gut.

Huh. Note to self. Keep working out.

When his demand didn't get the desired, immediate response, George growled as he glanced around the group. He must have finally noticed how Nicholas held Bodb's hand and Sandra held Maggie's. His eyes widened, then narrowed again.

"Are you responsible for this?" George snarled, pointing at Nicholas, then at Sandra. "You come here holding the hands of others?"

"This is what I wished to speak with you in your office about, Father," Attain tried once again. "You see, I'm already in a relationship." Smiling up at Ssimeas, he added, "We're going to Vegas to elope."

Once the words were out of his mouth, Attain suddenly really wanted to do just that. Despite the stressful situation, he grinned broadly. When Ssimeas smiled back, his deep gray eyes filled with warmth, Attain returned his attention to his father . . . only to find the man's face red with rage.

"If you do this, you're fired," George snarled. "You'll never—"

Before George could finish what Attain was certain would be a continuation of his threats, Brandon Alderman strode into the foyer, followed by Chrissy. "George, is everything okay?" He glanced around the group and buttoned his suit jacket. "I didn't realize this was going to be a large dinner party."

Chrissy's blue eyes lit up as she focused on Attain. "Attain! There you are." She began moving toward him, her arms outstretched as if to greet him with an embrace.

Attain took a step backward as Ssimeas edged partway in front of him.

Hesitating, Chrissy stopped. Her red-painted lips pursed into what could have been a confused pout, but Attain just thought she looked constipated. Glancing around the group, Chrissy folded her hands in front of her in a demure fashion even as her blue eyes took on a chilly look.

"Hi, Nicholas, Sandra. I didn't know you were coming." Chrissy's smile didn't warm her eyes. "How's married life?" She smirked as she peered pointedly at people's hands. "Must not be so good. Huh?"

Over the last week, Attain had learned that Sandra and Chrissy had stopped being *best friends* years before. It had been due to Sandra and Nicholas's mothers planning of the wedding that she'd ended up the maid of honor.

"Hi, Chrissy," Sandra greeted, her tone just as cool. "You're right. Nicholas and I have an annulment in the works. You remember Maggie, right?" Sandra didn't wait for an answer before adding, "She's going to be my wife, soon."

Nicholas grinned as he jumped in, saying, "And Bodb is going to be my husband." With a light chuckle, he added, "We're all going to Vegas. A triple wedding sounds like fun, doesn't it, Attain?" Nicholas nudged Attain's arm.

Attain opened his mouth to answer, but Chrissy surged forward with a squeal. Shoving past a clearly surprised Ssimeas, she grabbed Attain's upper arms as she pressed her breasts against his chest. "Is this your way of asking me to marry you?" As Chrissy leaned up, clearly intending to kiss him, she cried, "Oh, yes, Attain! Yes, yes!"

Gripping Chrissy's shoulders, Attain pushed her back as he retreated a couple of steps. "I'm sorry. No, Chrissy." When she tried to follow, he tightened his hold to keep her away from him. "I don't know what promises our fathers made about you and me, but I love another."

"Y-You've been ch-cheating on m-me?" Chrissy whimpered, her blue eyes filling with tears. "I-I never thought y-you of all p-people—" She didn't bother finishing her sentence. Instead, Chrissy sniffled as she took a step backward. "After everything Lucinda did to you? How could you do the same to me?"

Attain had to fight back a cringe upon hearing the name of his vindictive, cheating, ex-girlfriend from so many years before. He swallowed past the bile threatening to rise in his throat. Releasing her, Attain lifted his hands, palms out, in placation.

Forcing his voice to come out level and firm, Attain stated, "I didn't cheat on you, Chrissy, because we were never dating." He watched her jaw sag open and a look of denial cross her face. Hurrying onward, Attain stated forcefully, "Like I said, I don't know what promises our fathers made or what their plans were, but they weren't *my* promises." Waving his hand toward Ssimeas, who immediately wrapped his arm possessively around Attain's waist, he explained, "I'm in a relationship with Ssimeas."

Chrissy's cheeks flushed, and her eyes narrowed. "You're dating a guy? You're a fag?" Then her eyes cleared, and she shook her head. "No, you might be bisexual, but I know you've always dated women." Resting her hands on her hips, Chrissy frowned at him. "This better be a phase you get over damn quick, because I've waited a long time for you to get over your *I'm gonna be a bachelor forever* decision."

Attain just fought down his desire to roll his eyes. "No, Chrissy. I'm sorry. I just don't feel that way about you and never will." Reaching into the satchel he carried, he pulled out a folder. He stepped past her and held the folder out to his father. "I figured you'd have this attitude, so this is my resignation."

"You'll never work in law again, if you make this choice, Attain," George threatened.

"We'll see," Attain countered.

When George narrowed his eyes and didn't take the folder, Attain stepped left and placed it on a side table. "I sent a copy to Eliza and Jory," he said, referring to the firm's head of human resources as well as the third partner. "There's also an explanation as to why there's no notice. I'll clear out my desk in the morning." Then Attain turned and smiled at Ssimeas and his friends. "Thanks for coming with me and for the support."

Heading toward the door, Attain bid the others good-bye. He didn't miss the anger gleaming in George's eyes, or the chilly expression on Chrissy's face. The slight smile on Brandon's face and the man's small head nod, however, *that* surprised Attain.

Attain strode out the door, and his group headed to his *Avalanche*, but he handed the keys to Nicholas. His buddy lifted one brow but climbed behind the wheel without question. For the first time since he'd bought the vehicle years before, he climbed into the very back seat.

Ssimeas squeezed in beside Attain, stretching his long legs out between the two captains chairs that made up the middle row. Sandra and Maggie took those seats, while Bodb climbed into the front passenger seat. Attain snuggled into Ssimeas's side.

While Attain had expected exactly that outcome, it still hurt. His father had been the only family he had left.

"You're not alone, my mate," Ssimeas murmured into his ear before pressing a kiss to his temple.

"Of course not," Sandra immediately added. Reaching back, she squeezed his knee before taking Maggie's hand. "You have all of us."

Their support warmed Attain, and he smiled at them. "Thanks. That means a lot to me."

When they reached the ranch, Ssimeas took his hand and helped him from the *Avalanche*. He led him to a bedroom on the second floor that had been given to them. When Ssimeas began undressing him, massaging his limbs and touching each bit of exposed flesh along the way, Attain moved into his touches.

As they lay together, Attain welcomed Ssimeas's attention as he drove every thought but his gargoyle out of his mind.

True to his word, Attain arrived at the office bright and early. Ssimeas had tried to insist on joining him, but Attain had convinced him that his presence could do more harm than good. Attain had assured him that nothing would happen at the office, and Ssimeas had finally relented.

Several people dropped by his office once word got around that Attain was packing up and leaving.

Prissy had closed the door and stopped before the desk. With her hands on her hips, she had declared, "You better let me know when you have your new practice set up." Prissy pointed at him with one long, bright-yellow-colored nail and added, "And there better be a job waiting there for me."

Warming under her support, Attain grinned. "You know there will be."

"Damn skippy." Then Prissy had nodded and turned away. Before she opened the door, Attain was certain he heard her sniff and say, "Stupid, bigoted asshole." Then she'd returned to her desk.

Jory Dartmore arrived shortly afterward. He, too, closed the door. Settling in the chair before Attain's desk, he leaned back and rested his right ankle over his left knee.

Attain waited, meeting the man's serious, brown-eyed expression.

"You know, he can't fire you for who your partner is," Jory finally told him, cocking his head. "You don't have to leave."

Smiling a little, Attain leaned forward and folded his hands on his desk. "I know, but he can make my life difficult here." Attain shrugged. "Besides, I kinda like the idea of branching out on my own."

Nodding, Jory rose and held out his hand. "If you ever need anything."

Attain stood and shook Jory's hand. "Thank you."

After that, Jory left.

Attain managed to get everything in order by eleven o'clock. He said his good-byes to many of them, noticing George's closed door. Even his father's receptionist offered him a wave and a smile.

After unloading his things at his condo, Attain quickly changed into a pair of jeans and a polo shirt. He donned his leather jacket and helmet, shoved his wallet in his pocket, and grabbed his keys. With one thought in mind, Attain opened his garage door and swung onto his *Ducati*.

Eager to get back to Ssimeas, Attain roared away. He reached the highway and sped up. Anticipation thrummed through him.

Never in his wildest dreams would Attain have thought he would be so excited to get back to someone . . . and a man to boot. That didn't stop him from grinning behind the glass of his helmet. After taking the needed off-ramp, Attain spotted the large *BMW* behind him roaring closer at an alarming rate.

Attain's eyes widened as he spotted Chrissy behind the wheel through the glass. The look of rage etched on her features caused his heart rate to spike. Keeping an eye on her, Attain felt the hairs on his nape stand on end as she drew closer and closer.

It suddenly hit Attain.

She's gonna ram me or run me off the road.

Gunning his *Ducati's* engine, Attain sped up. At the same time, he used his helmet's *Bluetooth* connection to make a call.

CHAPTER TWELVE

Ssimeas missed Attain more than he thought possible, and it had only been four hours. Fortunately, the arrival of Maggie's grandmother, Lidia, offered a fantastic distraction. He greeted her with his hand outstretched. "It's nice to meet you. Welcome."

Lidia took his hand. Her brown-eyed gaze, so much like Maggie's, swept him up and down. "Likewise," she replied before releasing him.

For some reason, Ssimeas felt as if he'd been assessed in some manner.

Then Lidia focused on Bodb. She inclined her head, offering him a slight bow. "I am honored to meet an elder of the gargoyle race. Thank you for allowing me in your home."

"You are the grandmother of my extended family," Bodb replied, taking her hand and kissing it old-world style. "Of course, you are welcome." He smiled as he led her into the family room.

"May I be blessed to see your true forms?" Lidia asked, glancing between them.

"Grammy!" Maggie cried, clearly scandalized. Her cheeks even pinked. "You're not supposed to ask that."

Lidia blew a raspberry as she waved her other hand. "Don't be silly. When will I have another opportunity to see gargoyles?"

The short, slightly rotund man who'd been introduced as Artie chuckled lightly. "You know your grammy doesn't adhere to such stuffiness." The dark-haired man grinned widely as he pushed his glasses up his nose. "That's one of the reasons I love her so much." As Artie spoke, he tugged her away from Bodb and guided her a few steps toward the fireplace.

"It is fine, Maggie," Bodb replied, chuckling. "After all" — he waggled his eyebrows—"I have a request to make in return."

Lidia grinned, clapping her hands excitedly. "A little quid pro quo. Excellent."

Elder Bodb pulled his shirt from his back and kicked off his shoes and socks. Glancing Ssimeas's way, he lifted one brow. Realizing what his elder expected, Ssimeas quickly followed his lead.

Within a few seconds, they'd both shifted to their true forms.

"Oh, my," Lidia murmured, her tone filled with appreciation. She rounded them, clearly fascinated. "Stunning."

When Lidia reached out to touch Elder Bodb's wing, Maggie jumped forward and grabbed her wrist. "Um, taboo without permission," she explained when her grandmother peered at her with surprise in her eyes.

"That's true," Nicholas confirmed, rising from where he'd been relaxing on the love seat. "I'm Nicholas Lindson, owner and operator of the ranch, and I'm Elder Bodb's mate."

"Of course." After they shook, Lidia glanced between them. "So wings are sexual. I understand." She didn't seem the least bit embarrassed by her statement, although Nicholas's cheeks darkened a little. Instead, Lidia turned to Ssimeas. "Are horns also sexual? That they turn into your hair is absolutely fascinating."

"No, horns are not sexual," Ssimeas replied.

Ssimeas bent at the waist and bowed his head, allowing her to touch them. While Ssimeas loved having Nicholas grip his horns, it didn't arouse him. Instead, it was the fact that he used them to control him during sex that he got off on. Hell,

his horns were hard and sharp. He barely felt it when someone touched them.

"And tails?" Lidia asked brazenly as she pointed.

"Also sexual," Ssimeas told her, pleased that his dark skin
hid his discomfort.

Lidia nodded. She walked around them once more, openly,
brazenly staring as only an elderly lady could. The fact that
she looked to be in her early forties didn't change the fact that
they knew she'd lived for nearly two centuries.

As Lidia headed to the sofa and took a seat, Ssimeas ex-
changed an amused look with Elder Bodb. His leader
smirked, and his gray eyes twinkled. Then he crossed to the
love seat and pulled Nicholas down next to him.

Ssimeas chose a large recliner.

"I am so very pleased you are in such a safe environment,
Maggie," Lidia claimed, smiling at her granddaughter and
patting her hand. "You and your familiar will be well taken
care of." Then Lidia leaned over Maggie and patted Sandra's
thigh, since the four were seated on the long sofa together.
"It's lovely to see you again, dear. Congratulations on your
annulment."

Sandra laughed. "Thank you."

Ssimeas had heard the paperwork had finished processing,
and Sandra and Nicholas were both free to marry their actual
partners.

"So." Lidia turned and glanced between Elder Bodb and
Ssimeas. "What is it you need from me?"

Elder Bodb waved at Ssimeas, silently telling him to answer.

Sighing, Ssimeas explained, "Centuries ago, before we discovered that cinnamon could be used as birth control for gargoyles and their mates, we utilized the services of witches."
He leaned forward, drumming the claws of his right hand on
his knee. "They had a recipe for a brew that the gargoyle

could drink, a potion, I guess you'd call it, and it would do the same thing as cinnamon."

"If you have cinnamon, then why would you need this drink?" Lidia asked curiously, cocking her head.

"Although it is extremely rare, a few gargoyles are immune to the effects of cinnamon," Elder Bodb explained. He waved his way toward Ssimeas. "Ssimeas is one of those few."

"And Attain is allergic to cinnamon, so he can't take it either," Sandra explained further.

"Oh, and you've just gotten together, so he's not ready to get pregnant."

Lidia said it so nonchalantly, as if men carrying children was the most natural thing in the world. She hummed as she peered toward the ceiling, and her expression turned vacant. A moment later, Lidia blinked and smiled at him.

"I think I recall which potion you're referring to," Lidia claimed, nodding. "Although I've never made it, and I should double-check my notes from when I was training." Just as quickly, she turned to Maggie. "Oh, I bet you have your journals here. Why don't you go get the ones on brew-making?"

Maggie popped up. "I have them." She held out her hand to Sandra. "Wanna help me look."

"Sure." Sandra took Maggie's hand, and both women headed toward the door.

"Don't get distracted now, young lady," Lidia called behind them, although her tone held mirth, betraying that she teased.

Just as the door closed, Ssimeas's phone rang. He smiled when he pulled it from his pocket and saw Attain's number on the screen. "Hi, my mate," Ssimeas greeted warmly, eager to hear his mate's voice. "Are you on your way here?"

Yep, call me eager.

"I just got off the highway, and I'm on Sugarland Road heading toward the ranch, but Chrissy is behind me in her *BMW*, and I'm damn sure she's trying to run me off the road."

Ssimeas processed Attain's hurried ramblings in a heart-beat. With a roar, he leaped to his feet. "Attain's in trouble," he stated in answer to how Elder Bodb also rose. Returning his focus to his mate, he asked, "Are you on your *Ducati*?"

"Yeah. Want me to outrun her?" Attain offered. "I could. Figured you'd want to know."

Hearing the fear in Attain's voice, Ssimeas knew his mate had called him for a reason other than just to give him a heads up.

"Ssimeas, you can't go outside like that!" Elder Bodb roared, rushing after him.

Ssimeas just managed to hold in his snarl as his elder grabbed his shoulder, stopping him just before he opened the front door.

"We'll go out the back, Ssim," Nicholas told him. "All the hands who don't know about paranormals are in the south forty checking fences." He pointed over his shoulder. "Tell Attain to head to the hunting cabin. He'll know where I mean."

Nodding, Ssimeas relayed the message to Attain. "How far are you from there?" he couldn't help but ask.

"Mmm, twenty minutes." Attain hissed, and the sound of an engine revving sounded through the phone line. "God-dammit. Tell me Nicholas has the gate open."

Ssimeas hurried after Nicholas, rushing back through the house. "Nicholas. Attain is asking about a gate?"

Nicholas nodded. "I'll beat him to it," he assured as he sprinted to a shed that held their quads and tractors. "Bodb, take Ssimeas to the cabin. I'll meet you there." Then Nicholas hopped on a quad and roared away.

"Lebone, Sindrid, with us," Bodb ordered.

While Ssimeas couldn't even say when the other gargoyles had joined them, he would be grateful for all the help he could get. Of course, the idea of shredding Chrissy with his bare hands held a certain amount of appeal. After Ssimeas assured Attain that the gate would be open, he spread his wings and followed the others across a field and into the woods.

"Try to relax, Ssimeas," Lebone encouraged. "Attain will be fine. We won't let anything happen to him."

Ssimeas nodded.

What was there to say?

If anything ever happened to Attain, Ssimeas had no reason to live. He would go feral and need to be put down, or he would die of heartache.

A few minutes later, a small clearing opened up before him. A rustic log cabin dominated the space.

"To the trees," Elder Bodb ordered.

Ssimeas obeyed and landed on the limb of a tree. From his vantage point, he could see a good fifty yards down the road. Seeing the ruts and potholes, Ssimeas felt a seed of unease flood him.

Even with the view, Ssimeas heard the rev of engines first. He squinted down the road and spotted a plume of dust rising in the distance. Tensing, he couldn't stop his wings from twitching.

He desperately wanted to fly to Attain, pluck him from his bike, and wing him to safety. However, since he didn't know who might see while out on the road, he had to wait. Clutching the branch tighter, he damn near trembled with anticipation as the roar of engines grew louder.

"Wait until they enter the clearing," Bodb warned, his voice deep with authority. "Then you will be covered, and you may use whatever actions you deem necessary to secure your mate."

Ssimeas whipped his attention to his elder, and he spotted the angry gleam in his eyes. "Elder?" he whispered, surprised to see the feral light.

Elder Bodb gave him a toothy smile as he spread his slate

gray wings just enough to be taken as a sign of aggression. "If it were my mate being stalked by that bitch, I know how I would deal with it."

Hissing, Ssimeas nodded once, understanding.

Any way I see fit.

In the paranormal world, it was taboo to go after a mate. If a person tried it once, then they could try it again.

Ssimeas would never allow that to happen.

When Ssimeas returned his focus to the road, he spotted Attain on his *Ducati*. Due to the condition of the road, he wasn't going exceptionally fast. He was barely managing to stay ahead of the big, dark-red *BMW* bearing down on him. Ssimeas readied himself to jump.

Just as Attain reached the clearing, his front tire slid into a rut. His mate bobbled his motorcycle, and he went down. Skidding on his hip, Attain's body separated from the bike.

The *BMW* bore down on Attain.

Ssimeas leaped, landing on the hood of the vehicle, and dug his claws into the metal roofing. At the same time, Attain gained his feet and lurched toward the trees. Lebone swooped down and slammed his shoulder into the front left panel. A human-looking Sindrid grabbed Attain and helped him away from the now-shuddering vehicle.

"He's mine!"

Even through the windows and the metal of the *BMW*, Ssimeas still heard Chrissy's scream . . . which made no sense to him, since she'd just tried to run him over.

With Attain safe, at least for the moment, Ssimeas used his claws to peel back the roof like the lid of a sardine can. He had just enough presence of mind to shift back to his human form when he revealed Chrissy. She peered up at him, her mouth agape.

Chrissy recovered swiftly enough. "I'll kill you all!" she screamed, her icy blue eyes holding a manic gleam. Grabbing a gun that had been sitting in her cup holder, Chrissy lifted the weapon. "If I can't have him" — she pointed it in Attain's direction — "no one can!"

The report of the revolver echoed in Ssimeas's ears, almost drowning out the sound of the passenger window shattering.

Roaring in anger as Chrissy fired again, Ssimeas returned to his true form. The change must have drawn the blonde's attention, for she peered up at him and screamed. To Ssimeas's relief, she swung the weapon so she could point it at him.

Ssimeas never gave her the chance. Grabbing her wrist in a tight hold, he squeezed, controlling which direction she could point the gun even as she continued to discharge it. With a swipe of the claws on his other hand, he broke the seatbelt. Then he lifted Chrissy from the vehicle.

Standing on the ruined roof of the *BMW*, Ssimeas dangled a screaming, writhing Chrissy within his hold. "No one harms what is mine, human," he snarled, squeezing tighter. He felt the bones give way beneath his clawed hand and smelled the acrid scent of urine as Chrissy pissed herself. "You could have walked away, but now, you are *dead*."

Lifting his other hand, Ssimeas slashed it across her throat, silencing her screams. Then he swiped across her gut, spilling her intestines. Ssimeas finished by lacerating her torso, making certain he reached her heart.

Ssimeas watched with satisfaction as the feral gleam in her blue eyes faded. Smiling smugly, he heard her heart beat its last. Satisfied, Ssimeas dropped her unceremoniously back into the *BMW*'s now blood-splattered interior.

Then Ssimeas swept his gaze around the clearing. He spotted Attain standing near the tree-line, Sindrid at his side. Searching his mate's expression, he feared what he would see.

The life of an elder enforcer could sometimes be messy.

To Ssimeas's relief, a relieved smile curved Attain's pale face.

Jumping from the damaged vehicle, Ssimeas murmured, "Attain."

Attain rushed toward him, and Ssimeas wrapped his human in his arms. Holding him tightly, he drank in his mate's fantastic scent. While undertones of fear still lingered, it was fading quickly. To Ssimeas's surprise, he smelled arousal and need.

Moaning, Ssimeas felt his own body answering, his blood flowing south and filling his dick. "Are you okay?" he asked, nuzzling his mate's temple, then lowering his mouth to his neck, he licked up the tendon.

"I'm okay," Attain assured, rubbing up and down his back. "Thank you for coming."

"I will always come." Then Ssimeas lifted his head and peered down at him. "Although I would prefer you stay safe and this doesn't happen again."

Attain grinned widely at him. "I'll try." Then his mirth faded, and his gaze strayed to the car. "I know why you had to kill her, but what happens now?"

"We'll take care of it. Nothing will come back to us," Elder Bodb assured, crossing to stop next to them. He offered an encouraging smile. "Why don't you head off, Ssimeas, and make certain your mate is safe and well."

More than on board with that idea, Ssimeas nodded. "Thank you, Elder."

Sweeping Attain into his arms, Ssimeas spread his wings. He jumped, soaring into the air. Attain laughed, clutching him.

Ssimeas loved the feel of his mate in his arms, laughing, safe, and happy. His cock throbbed, so he headed to a secluded location on the ranch. He had every intention of exploring every inch of his man.

When Ssimeas landed in the meadow by the river, he laid Attain on the bed of soft grass and peered into his mate's eyes.

"You're mine, Attain," he whispered. "All mine." Then Ssimeas growled softly and licked up his neck. "I need you, my mate. Need to feel you."

Attain grinned and nodded. "I'd say fuck me and make yourself feel better, but we don't have any condoms."

"I have one," Ssimeas revealed. "But soon we won't need them."

"Oh really?" Attain rubbed his hands up and down Ssimeas's torso, setting his nerve endings on fire. "How do you figure?"

"Maggie's grandmother, Lidia, arrived today," Ssimeas revealed as he began stripping Attain of his clothes. "She is very skilled and will make me a brew that will render me infertile." Holding Attain's gaze, he assured, "I will drink it every day for the rest of life, or until you say otherwise."

Attain's smile turned soft as he rubbed up his neck and massaged his tendons. "You're a thief. Did you know that?"

Ssimeas lifted one brow. "Really? How so?"

Nodding once, Attain stated, "You stole this bachelor's heart."

"You stole mine first," Ssimeas countered, pecking a kiss to his lips. "Love you."

"Love you, too." Then Attain grinned widely. "Got lube?"

Laughing, Ssimeas nodded. "Yep. Elder Bodb recommended I always be ready."

"Oh, damn," Attain murmured, his voice turning rough. "Fuck me, my gargoyle. I need you, too."

Ssimeas ever-so-happily obeyed.

You may also enjoy the following from eXtasy Books Inc:

With a Gentle Nudge
Charlie Richards

Excerpt

Finishing his shower, Pierce decided to give a friendly warning to Anthony. His fuck-buddy deserved to know that some of his customers were homophobes. He knew his friend was deep in the closet. Anthony didn't want his sexual orientation to impact his business.

Pierce dried swiftly, then slung the damp towel back around his waist. Carrying his shower supplies, he returned to his locker. He spotted Anthony waiting for him, a clipboard in hand.

"I filled out everything for you, so you just need to sign the bottom," Anthony told him softly after a glance around. "Figured it'd be easier for you."

Smiling in appreciation, Pierce murmured, "Thanks, Anth." Then he swept his gaze over the space, too, before opening his locker. Lowering his voice further, he whispered, "Wanted to warn you. Bill is a homophobe." Seeing the way Anthony's brows shot up in obvious question, Pierce added, "He's said some shit to me."

Anthony's face paled a little. "How the hell would he even know about you?"

Pierce shrugged his wide shoulders. "No idea." The gym had been his safe place, but that seemed to be changing. "Just thought I'd give you a heads up."

Taking the clipboard, Pierce stared at the form on it. He took in the lines that formed boxes and the letters that were supposed to be words. Pierce took a deep breath and let it out slowly.

The more worked up he was, the harder it was for him to comprehend what he was seeing.

"You just need to sign here." Anthony pointed near the bottom.

Pierce nodded as he settled on one of the wooden benches that ran the length of the locker bay. Resting the clipboard on his thighs, he placed the tip of the pen where Anthony had indicated. After another calming breath, Pierce painstakingly wrote his name.

He took another few minutes to work out most of the words on the form. As much as he trusted Anthony, he didn't want to be too dependent on him. After confirming where he needed to be and when, he handed the pen and board back to Anthony.

"Thanks, Anth." Pierce stood and grabbed his clean clothes from his locker. "I think I'm gonna go for a run."

Anthony's snort drew Pierce's attention to his friend's grinning face. "You just showered, and you're gonna go work out some more?"

Pierce shrugged.

"You could have just run on the treadmill," Anthony pointed out, using a thumb to point over his shoulder.

"Naw," Pierce told him. "Not that kind of run." Grinning, he pulled his jeans on underneath his towel. Then he dropped the damp fabric as he zipped and buttoned. "Ready to get out in nature and get some fresh air."

After another nod, Anthony turned and waved the clip-board. "Have fun."

Pierce grunted in acknowledgment as he pulled his gray wife-beater over his head. After pulling on his socks and shoes, he picked up his bag and headed out of the gym. Feeling the warm sun's rays on his cheeks coupled with the cool spring breeze, he grinned.

Yeah. Nature it is.

Opening his soft-top's door, Pierce climbed into his Jeep. He tossed his bag into the back and shut the door. Firing up the engine, he headed north.

Even though Pierce had just worked his arms on the bag, he still felt energized. He always seemed to have an excess of energy. The physical activity kept him from never getting any sleep. He'd struggled with that as a kid, since school forced him to sit in a chair and listen to a teacher drone on and on for hours at a time—then the time spent doing homework.

Dismissing a past Pierce had no ability to change, Pierce turned his Jeep onto a county road leading into the hills. He thought it was a little ironic that he'd ended up a receptionist for the town's police station. Sheriff Stillwell was understanding however, and he had bought Pierce a desk that he could raise and lower, allowing him to stand while doing his work.

The sheriff didn't even mind that Pierce danced while working. The man smiled or chuckled occasionally, but the noise was never malicious. He said as long as the work was done correctly, Pierce could do it however he wanted.

Finding the little-used trailhead he wanted, Pierce turned onto it. He parked, noticing a number of motorcycles in the lot. Peering over them, he wondered what it would feel like to ride on one. Pierce had a soft-top Jeep with roll-bars, and he figured it would feel similar to when he removed the canvas.

With that thought, another bounced through Pierce's mind. It was almost warm enough to do just that.

Maybe when I get home.

Oh, I should check the forecast, first.

After slipping from his vehicle, Pierce reached in and grabbed a light jacket from the back. He tied the arms around his waist, then shut the door. Since it was a little cooler in the hills, he wanted it just in case.

"Oh. And water and a couple of granola bars," Pierce reminded himself. He rounded his vehicle and opened the passenger door. After snagging a satchel from the floorboard, he grabbed the granola bars from the glove box and a couple bottles of water from the case of them he kept in the back. "And we're ready."

Pierce figured a shrink would have a field day with the fact that he talked to himself, but he didn't give a shit.

Heading up the trail, Pierce swung his arms, stretching his shoulders, biceps, and triceps as he started his hike. He hadn't gone far when he realized he heard voices. Figuring it was the guys who had been on the motorcycles, Pierce glanced around with interest.

When Pierce rounded the next bend, he noticed a flash of yellow between two trees to his right. He paused and squinted, peering into the gloom. It took him a second, but he realized someone was over there.

Pierce glanced at the trail, nibbling his bottom lip. The rules of hiking were to stay on the trail, but he knew a lot of people had picnics, too. Just as he turned, deciding it was none of his business, Pierce saw a face between the branches . . . and it was someone he knew.

"Deputy Anderson," Pierce murmured, heading in that direction. The man, Mac to his friends, had recently retired when he'd found the love of his life in a cute twinky guy named Deter. Pierce had thought they'd left the area.

Is that really him?

Lifting a branch, Pierce eased through a break in the trees. "Hey, Deputy Anderson," he called, grinning at the man. When the guy turned, Pierce lifted his hand in greeting as he moved into the clearing. "Hi, there! I didn't know you were back in town."

Deputy Anderson's eyes widened, and his lips parted, his surprise etched over his features. "Pierce." He darted his gaze around the area as he strode toward him. "Hey, man. How are you?"

Pierce opened his mouth to answer, but an odd popping and cracking sound drew his attention. Focusing left, he gaped as he stumbled backward a step. There . . . right before his eyes . . . was the oddest damn thing he'd ever seen.

"Th-There was a zebra . . . and now he's a man!"

Lifting his hands in placation, Deputy Anderson stepped before him, blocking his view of the naked, blushing male. "Pierce, just calm down. Take a breath." He rested his hands on Pierce's shoulders and squeezed lightly. "I can explain."

Staring at his ex-co-worker, Pierce cried, "How the hell can you explain that?"

ABOUT THE AUTHOR

Charlie started writing fantasy when she was eight, and after stumbling onto her first erotic romance at age nineteen, she realized her true calling. She now focuses on writing gay erotic romance, normally of the paranormal variety, with heroes of all kinds. With the help and support of her husband, Charlie finally fulfilled one of her life-long goals . . . move to acreage with her horses. You can often find her curled up with her laptop and a cup of tea or glass of wine, creating her next adventure. Charlie enjoys exploring the mountains of her new Oregon home on horseback, 4-wheeler, or motorcycle.

She can be reached at ch.richards2010@yahoo.com

Or visit her at www.charlie-richards.com

www.ingramcontent.com/pod-product-compliance
Lightning Source LLC
Chambersburg PA
CBHW060639130626
46555CB00002B/877